The King's Mission

July - August 1941

A Misfit Squadron Novel

Simon Brading

ISBN: 978-1-917470-07-0

PROLOGUE

30th July 1941

Dozens of sailors stood with their backs against the cold metal of the corridors and bulkheads in the semi darkness of the *HMS Beagle*. The undersea boat was rising through the water, approaching the surface, and the currents around them were getting stronger, making the deck shift and roll, but they swayed with it easily, all well used to the way it moved. After fourteen days of inactivity, running silent on a secret mission, they were more than eager to spring into action, but they remained quiet, patiently waiting for the order.

Two women in the bridge area weren't quite so accustomed to the unpredictable motions, though. It was their first voyage in an undersea boat and they were forced to clutch at the chart table in the middle of the bridge area to maintain their balance.

The taller of the two, Kitty Wright, a beautiful young blonde with Lieutenant's stripes on the sleeves of her Royal Aviator Corps dress uniform jacket, grimaced as a particularly sharp lurch almost knocked her off her feet. 'When the king gave us this mission, did you imagine it would be like this?'

Her companion, Gwen Stone, turned her green eyes to her, but there was no chance for an answer to be given, or heard, because chaos broke out on all sides when the boat gave one last sickening plunge as it breeched the surface and the deck levelled off beneath them.

At a nod from the captain, standing with the pilots at the chart table, the petty officers stationed by the ladders began shouting, chivvying

"

their charges up the ladders as hatches were thrown open and the first daylight any of them had seen in days poured in. Four dozen sailors had to get up only three ladders, but they were well drilled and the process took less than a minute and then only the two women, the captain, and the few crew members who had to stay below to pilot the vessel, were left down below.

The captain waited until the pounding of the footsteps on the deck overhead had faded away completely, then turned his bearded and grizzled face to the RAC officers.

'Well?' he asked, impatiently. 'Shall we?'

Without waiting for an answer, he went to the nearest ladder and started up, climbing rapidly and easily, despite his advancing years.

The women rolled their eyes, then hurried after him.

Throughout the journey, Captain Arthur Birkbreach, a veteran of the First Great War and one of the most highly decorated undersea boat officers the Royal Navy had ever had, had let them know whenever he possibly could that he would much rather be hunting the Prussians than providing a taxi service. He was fully aware of how important the mission was and had received his orders directly from the king, but that didn't stop him complaining and grumbling about how an older undersea boat would have been more suited to the task than the Beagle, which had been launched less than a month before and was one of the Kingdom of Great Britain's most fearsome naval weapons.

Gwen eyed the rungs warily and tucked her voluminous skirts and petticoats between her legs before following him, far more slowly and warily. She emerged into bright sunlight, blinding after so long stuck in a tin can, and made her way to the railing of the conning tower. She positioned herself next to the captain and gazed around in wonder, completely forgetting to stand at attention like she'd been briefed.

Kitty came up beside her and chuckled. 'Close your mouth, darling! And no, this definitely isn't *anything* like how I imagined it.'

The American didn't make any more attempt to stand at attention than Gwen, however, unlike her fellow pilot, she didn't gape at the huge buildings looming up in front of them, rather she smiled up at the statue on the island they were passing. 'Hi, there, Libby. I'm home.'

CHAPTER 1

Captain Birkbreach had been given orders to remain undetected and they had spent most of the journey below the waves, only surfacing in the middle of the night for an hour or so to check their position, rewind the springs and get some fresh air. It had been a surprise, then, when a coded message had been received the night before, instructing them to enter the harbour at midday, instead of under the cover of darkness as had originally been planned. It had been even more of a surprise to find tens of thousands of people waiting for them.

The British undersea boat had surfaced well within New York harbour, a hundred yards or so beyond Liberty Island, and found it filled to capacity with all kinds of vessels, both military and civilian. Two fast patrol boats had moved in to escort the Beagle as soon as it had appeared, but they could do nothing to prevent the boats, ferries, launches, dinghies and even canoes filled with people who were laughing, cheering and waving flags, both the British Union Flag and the American Rising Star, from cruising right up to within yards of it. The mayhem didn't end on the sea, either, because there were also all manner of aircraft flying overhead. Conventional aircraft banked and looped around several airships and sometimes swooped down to within fifty yards or less of the water, but none of them seemed to come anywhere near to colliding. Gwen shaded her eyes to gaze up at them, trying to work out how they were dancing around each other safely, whether they were being coordinated in some way or whether it was just the skill of the pilots. However, Kitty's elbow in her side reminded her that she was supposed to be behaving in a military fashion for once and she reluctantly dragged her eyes back to the horizon. That wasn't such a bad thing, though, because it was an extremely impressive horizon for her to contemplate.

Much of the island of Manhattan, where they were headed, was covered with buildings, what the Americans called "skyscrapers". In their case it wasn't an inaccurate term as most of the ones she could see were taller than the Brunel Tower of Buckingham Palace, the tallest building in the whole of the Kingdom of Britain. The majority were brick or stone, but a few were steel and glass concoctions and there were a couple of silvery metal ones, shining brilliantly. Some were capped with radio towers, others had clocks, and there were even airship mooring masts on a few, although Gwen couldn't imagine how dangerous it had to be to try to land one so high, with the winds and unpredictable air currents swirling around above the artificial canyons of the streets. No two buildings were alike, though, and no matter how hard Gwen tried she could find no rhyme or reason to their organisation. It was if whoever was responsible for putting them up had just done whatever they felt like at the time, or, perhaps, what they'd had the money for.

Discordant, angry noises drew her attention away from her contemplation of the architecture and she frowned at a large motorboat off the ship's starboard bow. Not only was it pumping out noxious black smoke, evidence of it being powered by an internal combustion engine, but it was also filled to the brim with people who were gesticulating at them, waving placards and chanting angrily.

Now that she took proper notice she could see that there were actually a few vessels in the bay carrying people who were not very welcoming of the visitors, however, they were in a vast minority and their shouts were being completely drowned out.

Gwen's knowledge of American history had been sketchy at best and she had thought it would be a good idea to brush up on it a bit before arrival, so that was one of the things she and Kitty had done through the long hours of the voyage, most of them spent in their tiny, and not very private, cabin. Even with so much time on their hands, it wasn't possible for Kitty to give her more than a basic overview of the Federation, like a brief history of the countries that made it up, what each contributed, the political views of its people and what they did for fun. Most of it Gwen knew she wouldn't need and didn't worry too much about, but there was one thing that Kitty told her that stuck in her mind - she told her that there were quite a few people in the United

Federation that were not very keen on the British and wouldn't be particularly friendly during their visit.

The problems between the two nations had begun with the war for independence, but that was centuries ago and forgotten by all but the most dyed-in-the-wool American patriots.

There had been another war, less than fifty years ago, right before the Federation had been formed. The Americans wanted the entire continent to form part of their new country, but Britain had naturally refused to hand over the Canadian Dominion - the Canadians hadn't been too keen on the idea either, wanting to remain British. The United States, Venezuela, Mexico and Peru had declared war and marched their troops across the border into Canada.

The "soft-boiled egg war" as it was known in Britain lasted three minutes. The only casualties sustained before smarter heads in the soon to be Federation prevailed were two deer who had been in the wrong place at the wrong time. The troops had gone home, the Federation had been formed without truly unifying the continent, and the deer had ended up on Canadian plates. Since then there had been a few fights between Canada and America over fishing rights as well as a couple of drunken incursions by Americans, but nothing major and it was only really the people living in the north of the Federation along the border who cared about any of that.

There was, however, one thing, one bone of contention that was guaranteed to rile up many Americans, no matter where they came from. It wasn't anything physical, like a border, and it had nothing to do with the continuous battle to get the Federation to abandon its use of polluting combustion engines. It was more intangible in nature, more philosophical, but no less important to some people - *religion*.

When Empress Victoria had dissolved the Church of England and declared the Enlightenment it had been in an attempt to remove one of the greatest sources of hatred and intolerance in the world, banish superstition, and usher in an age of reason. However, despite one of the key tenets of the Enlightenment being one of tolerance, that everyone could continue to believe what they wanted, many deeply religious people around the world had seen it as an attack.

She couldn't quite make out what the passengers in the boat were chanting, over the noise the people on the other vessels were making, but she didn't need to; the placards they were brandishing were clear enough - they accused the British of being godless and warmongering and told them in a not particularly polite way to go home.

She put the protesters out of her mind, after all, there were always going to be people who were in disagreement with anything, and turned her gaze to where the Beagle was headed.

They had been directed to dock at Battery Park, near the southern tip of the island. It had one of the oldest piers still in use and, according to Kitty, was where immigrants had arrived in the last century. Whether or not the Americans were making some kind of statement by using this particular pier, nobody on the Beagle could work out, but they had certainly laid out the red carpet for their guests.

'They don't do things by half measures do they?' Gwen said out of the side of her mouth.

Kitty smirked. '*They*, darling? *I'm* one of these people, remember?'

'I know.' Gwen answered, grinning. 'But I hope you've been in Britain long enough for us to give you a better sense of what is vulgar.'

The American sized up the reception that had been prepared for them. 'Well, they *might* have gone a *little* bit overboard...'

Three large grandstands had been constructed in a semi-circle overlooking the end of pier and, like the boats, they were packed with spectators, quite a few of whom were waving flags. There were flags everywhere, in fact - they draped the grandstands and the small dais that had been built in front of them, they hung on flagpoles throughout the park and lined the pier, there were even a couple that had to be fully fifty feet long hanging on the nearby buildings. From what photographs Gwen had seen of the parades Americans like to throw, it was normal for them to plaster flags everywhere, but she was fairly sure that she'd never seen so many Union Flags in one place before. Not even during Emperor George's coronation.

As soon as the mooring ropes touched the land, a brass band of at least a hundred pieces broke out into the British national anthem. At the same time, a specially constructed gangplank, also, of course, hung with flags and streamers, was swung into place against the conning tower. Kitty, as the guest of honour for this first public appearance of the two pilots, led Gwen and Captain Birkbreach down it and onto American soil.

There was a welcoming committee waiting for them, all six of them men, but three stood out for their obvious sense of self-importance and they stepped forwards to greet the new arrivals to the clicking and whirring of the cameras of a whole troop of photographers. The sour-looking elderly man in the middle of the trio, who was wearing a sombre black suit and top hat as if he were at a funeral, rather than the lighter grey and blue suits and bare heads of the others, nodded to

Gwen and the captain before turning to Kitty. Gwen thought she saw his lip curl slightly in something like disdain as he looked down his nose at her, but then he broke out into a smile. It was a politician's smile, though, and she felt an instant dislike for the man, which only deepened as he addressed Kitty in a rather condescending tone.

'Miss Wright, I am Wilberforce Gould, Senator for the State of New York, and in the name of the United Federation of American States I have the pleasure of welcoming you back to the land of your birth.'

He held out his hand for Kitty to shake and Gwen smothered a smirk when she didn't even look at it. Instead, she left it hanging while she saluted smartly, lingering a tad longer than she needed to, and only then reaching to take it.

Gould's smile wavered when she merely squeezed his hand for a second then released it, but he recovered quickly and gestured at his companions. 'This is Mayor Winston and Governor Bostwick.'

The smiles of those two gentlemen, both in their late fifties, were far more genuine as they stepped forwards to take Kitty's hand in turn. She gave them far briefer salutes, but only so as not to keep them waiting longer than necessary and shook their hands warmly.

Once that was done they were joined by the other three men, who hastily introduced themselves as the port admiral, the head of the New York City business association and the aide to the senator, and together they climbed onto the dais. The senator gestured perfunctorily at the chairs lined up at the rear of the platform, then went to stand at a microphone, facing the audience.

Gwen shared a look with Kitty before taking the chair next to her and preparing herself for a long and boring afternoon.

The senator spoke for a full hour, but there was very little to do with Kitty or the British visit in his speech, instead he used the opportunity to talk about himself. Kitty was due to speak next, but when the senator went to his seat she didn't move. Lucky, Gwen realised that she had dozed off and nudged her in the ribs to wake her before anyone noticed. She didn't blame Kitty in the slightest; if she hadn't had to sit through dozens of far more tedious speeches while at Société Aéronautique meetings she might have fallen asleep too. It looked like quite a few in the crowd had, actually.

When they'd found out that they would be making a big entrance instead of the quiet one they'd expected, Gwen and Kitty had retired to their cabin to work on a speech for the American. In the few hours they'd had they'd been able to come up with something they thought everyone would be happy with - the British because it expressed the purpose of the visit, the Americans because she told them how pleased she was to be home, and the crowd because it was full of humour and short. The contrast with the senator's speech couldn't have been more drastic and following him, at least in Gwen's opinion, cast Kitty in a more positive light than if she'd just addressed the crowd on her own.

After she finished, to far more applause than the senator, the Mayor and Governor made short speeches welcoming the British delegation, then the band struck up again, this time with the American anthem - "The Rising Star Forever", by John Philip Sousa. Hands were shaken once more, photographs were posed for, then the party descended from the dais.

The senator immediately stalked away to his autocar, but the other dignitaries spared a few moments to welcome the pilots more informally before making their way to their own vehicles. Captain Birkbreach waited impatiently until all the politicians had gone before saying his own goodbyes. He was taking the Beagle to resupply before meeting them in Caracas, the American capital, for the return journey. They saluted him smartly, to more clicking and whirring of cameras, then he did a smart about turn and stomped up the gangplank to his boat.

'Squadron Leader? Aviator Lieutenant?'

The pilots turned to find a dark-haired young man in an extremely well-tailored dark blue three-piece suit standing only a few feet from them. Even if it hadn't been for his rather upper class accent, they would have had no trouble telling he was British by the fact that he was leaning nonchalantly on an umbrella, even though there wasn't a cloud in the summer sky.

'Where on earth did you come from?' Kitty asked, peering around almost comically in an attempt to work out where he'd sprung from.

The man waved away her question with a chuckle. 'I'm the consul's aide - it's my job to remain unobtrusive. Now, if you would come with me, please, the autocar is waiting.'

He took them to a black autocar with small British flags on the wings of its bonnet, parked with the ones the American dignitaries were now getting into and opened the rear door for them. He followed them in, taking the rear-facing chair, and tapped on the partition between them and the driver with the curved wooden handle of his umbrella.

The autocar pulled away smoothly and Gwen peered out with interest as they left Battery Park behind and turned onto one of the main thoroughfares that ran the length of Manhattan Island.

New York had long been known as a place where dreams could come true and where everyone was welcome and free to be whoever they wanted to be. It was said to be one of the most exciting cities in the world, with entertainments for any taste and enough going on to keep one busy for a lifetime.

What she could see through the window seemed to put the lie to that, though.

The buildings immediately adjacent to the park were grey and uninspiring blocks, unrelieved by decoration or colour and the people trudging along about their business, going in and out of them, were equally lifeless. Most of them were dressed in severe dark suits, almost as if it were a uniform they had to wear, and they were barely interacting with each other. They certainly didn't have the look of people who were fulfilling their dreams and she wondered how they could bear to spend their working lives in such dour surroundings.

The vehicles sharing the road with the autocar didn't help matters either. The majority were heavy lorries moving freight from the docks and their internal combustion engines were belching so much black smoke into the air that the pollution rivalled that of London at the turn of the century, before hydrogen substituted coal in things like vehicles, homes and electrical production.

She wrinkled her nose and turned her eyes upwards, curious whether the aircraft, which hadn't stopped buzzing around overhead during the speeches, were still there. She was unfamiliar with many of the models she'd spotted, especially among the fixed-wing aircraft, and wanted to get a better look at them while she wasn't constrained by propriety. However, even though the road was wide, the skyscrapers bordering it on both sides were huge and, no matter how she craned her neck, or pressed her face to the window, she couldn't see the sky except for too brief glances between buildings.

Disappointed, she gave up, but there was a pleasant surprise in store for her when she brought her gaze back down. Without her realising it, at some point during the short time she'd been distracted the autocar had moved into what looked like an affluent residential area, where far more care had be taken to make the street pleasant. Tall trees lined both sides, providing shelter from the midday sun, and plants and flowers hung on the balconies of the buildings, their cheerful colours relieving the monotony of the buildings. The filthy lorries had gone too - they must have turned off somewhere, because now there were only small vehicles beside them. Most were four- or five-seater passenger vehicles, much like the ones that could be seen on the streets of English cities, but there were also quite a few smaller spring-powered sports autocars weaving in and out of the slower traffic and even a few highly streamlined vehicles bearing the lightning bolt logo of Nikola Tesla's electrical autocar manufacturer on their bonnets. She was curious about the latter in particular, but she couldn't get a proper look at one of them from a moving vehicle, so she turned her attention to the people on the pavements. They were very different here than they had been in the district next to the park. For a start, they were far more cheerful and in far less of a hurry as they strolled along in the cool shade, went in and out of the boutiques, cafés and restaurants, or browsed the wares of street vendors. Also, while quite a few were in similar clothing to what you would see on the streets of any other city in the world, or sombre dark suits, many were dressed in what the British would have called their "Sunday best" (or at least they would have done half a century or more ago, during Empress Victoria's reign). Corsets, petticoats and parasols, in a dizzying array of colours, were apparently the style of the day for women, while the men were equally flamboyant, in top hats and long coats in bright tones or embroidered with complex patterns. There were children too, not just infants with their parents, but whole groups of them, of all ages, in smart school uniforms, out visiting the various museums and churches in the area, she supposed.

Here, then, was the New York that featured in so many books, movies and songs, with everyone going about their day seemingly without a care in the world and with art and entertainment their principal occupation and motivation.

It was as if the war didn't exist and Gwen supposed that for them it didn't; it was thousands of miles and a continent away. There was no need for the austerity that had overpowered much of British culture and no need for Americans to forgo the pleasures and excesses of the past couple of decades since the First Great War.

'You are such a tourist.'

Gwen laughed as she dragged herself away from the view and smiled at Kitty, who squeezed her hand and smiled back.

'Is this your first time in New York, Squadron Leader?'

The smile dropped instantly from the faces of both the pilots and they turned to face the young man. Misfit Squadron had always had its opponents and detractors, many of whom spoke exactly the same way as the young man, with a languid, dismissive tone, an upper class accent and a condescending sneer firmly in place. Since the squadron had been forcibly disbanded, the criticisms had only worsened, especially from the War Minister and his cronies who saw an opportunity to further consolidate their power.

There was no sneer on the man's face, though. Instead, surprisingly, there was genuine interest.

'Uh, actually, no,' she said, 'I've been here once before.'

Kitty shook her head. 'Was there an aeronautical society meeting here by any chance?'

'How did you guess?' Gwen poked her tongue out her, but retracted it immediately when she remembered they had an audience. She cleared her throat and looked back at the young man. 'I was only three when I came here for the Société Aéronautique meeting, so I don't exactly remember much.'

He nodded seriously. 'Then I will endeavour to find some time for you to see the sights while you're here.'

'Thank you, Mr...?'

The man's eyes widened. 'Oh, I'm terribly sorry, how remiss of me.' He leaned forward and stuck out a hand. 'Johnathon Gascoyne-Beresford, of the London Gascoyne-Beresfords, don't you know?'

Kitty took his hand. 'No, I'm afraid I really don't.'

Gwen snorted in amusement, but Gascoyne-Beresford just took it in his stride.

'Our families must not move in the same circles, then, Lieutenant. Our loss, I'm sure.'

He smiled at her, then shook Gwen's hand before sitting back in his seat and going on as if he hadn't been interrupted. 'I am the aide to Lady Rosemary Cooper, His Majesty's Consul here in Manhattan. Her ladyship apologises that she could not come to welcome you in person, but sends her warmest greetings and is looking forward to meeting you later. She has put me *entirely* at your disposal while you are here, so, if there is anything at all I can do, then don't hesitate to ask. Oh, and *please* call me John, everybody does.' He smiled at them again, then took a red folder from the seat beside him and pulled out a couple of sheets of paper, which he handed to them. 'Here are your itineraries for the next week. There's no need to go through them in detail right now, but essentially you have the next four days filled with dinners, talks and various publicity events in the local area. Then, on Sunday, we fly down to Caracas, where there will be more of the same, but Lieutenant Wright will also be addressing both the Federal Congress and Senate.'

'I'm doing what, now?' Kitty glared at him. 'I didn't sign up for that!'

The young man's eyebrows rose. 'The whole reason you're here is to persuade your countrymen to enter the war on our side.' He gestured at the pieces of paper that Gwen and Kitty had on their laps. 'The luncheons, press conferences, publicity events and such will go a long way to doing that by convincing the populace that ours is a just fight and they in turn will put pressure on the politicians who represent them. That won't be enough, though. We have to go directly to the men and women who will actually be casting their votes in a couple of weeks' time. So you will stand up in front of both houses and tell them exactly what is happening in Europe and what it would mean for the world, and therefore America, if Prussia were allowed to prevail. The Ambassador and everyone else on His Majesty's staff over here have explained why they should help us until they're blue in the face, but they've never heard it from one of their own and that might make all the difference.' He smiled. 'Don't worry, it'll be a cinch. You have the personality and the looks to charm a bunch of jaded old men and we have some damn good speeches prepared for you.'

'Well, that's alright then...'

Kitty rolled her eyes at Gwen, who smirked.

'And, as for you, Squadron Leader,' the aide said.

Gwen turned to him in alarm. 'As for me what?'

'While you won't be addressing the American government, your contribution will be no less important. You have an international reputation, not just for your piloting skills, but as a brilliant mind as well. So, you will be both representing the highest ideals of Britain as one of our best and brightest and showing this rather backwards country that a woman can fight just as well as a man.' He grimaced. 'One of the biggest stumbling blocks we have come up against is that the vast majority of Americans are aghast at the way we have women fighting and dying for their country. That fact has often been used against us as an example of how callous and unfeeling we are. Much worse than the "god-fearing Prussians". Even some of the politicians who are on our side have said that their vote is conditional on women being taken off the front lines.'

He held up a hand to forestall the protests that were immediately springing to both of the pilot's lips. 'Obviously we can't do that.' He smiled. 'Not only would that reduce our combat effectiveness considerably, but we would likely have a revolt on our hands.'

'Damn right,' Kitty stated, nodding emphatically.

Gwen scowled. 'And how am I supposed to go about convincing all these people that I can fight just as well as a man? Pick fights?'

Gascoyne-Beresford shook his head. 'Nothing so barbaric, although I'm sure you'd put up a good showing and I know quite a few of the politicians we're trying to recruit would rather enjoy watching something like that. No, we've actually got a couple of things that are rather more up your street for you to do, starting tomorrow morning with a visit to the brand new flagship of the American Navy, an aircraft carrier by the name of the, uh...' he glanced down at his copy of their itinerary, 'the *UFS Machu Pichu*. It's currently at a pier a short way up the Hudson River on the west side of the island, not far from where you landed, actually. You'll be flying one of their new aircraft, a Choice Aviation Company *Corsario*, off the carrier, putting it through its paces, then being interviewed by the press afterwards. The Americans want you to sing the aircraft's praises, obviously, and I suggest you do, even if you would rather say something else about it.' He glanced down at his paper again. 'A couple of days after that, on Saturday, we'll be heading down to Philadelphia for their air show.' He gave her a knowing smile. 'They only want you to do a couple of passes for the crowds, but I think it'd be a good chance to show them what a British pilot can do, don't you?'

Gwen grinned. 'Absolutely.'

Kitty pouted. 'Why does she get to have all the fun? Can't I play around in the aircraft while she stands up in front of the politicians?'

The aide gave her a crooked smile. 'I'm afraid not, Lieutenant. But don't worry, she's not getting away lightly. In the next few days, Squadron Leader Stone has three brunches with various women's societies and will be expected to give short, but inspiring speeches at each of them.'

The news cheered Kitty up no end, while Gwen groaned, slumping in her seat. 'I think I'd rather go up in front of the politicians.' She blinked as something occurred to her and sat up straight again. 'Hang on a moment. Some of these things must have taken days, if not weeks, to organise. Why did we have to sneak out of England and spend ten days under the water with no daylight if everyone knew we were coming? Wasn't this supposed to be a secret mission?'

Gascoyne-Beresford tilted his head and raised an eyebrow quizzically. 'Well, the mission only really needed to be secret to begin with. Once you were safely over this side of the pond there was no point and besides, we didn't want to miss such a golden opportunity for you to make a grand entrance, did we?'

For the past couple of minutes or so the autocar had been driving alongside Central Park and it now pulled off the road and into the drive of a building, coming to stop in front of a large glass door flanked by brushed silver pillars.

Gwen frowned as she read the bronze plaque on the brick wall of the building. 'The A.C. Hotel Fifth Avenue? I thought we would be staying at the consulate?'

'That was the original plan, but...'

The aide was interrupted by Kitty, who let out a very uncharacteristically girlish squeal and burst out of the vehicle, almost knocking over the blue-liveried man who had come to open the door for them.

'Nicky!'

Gascoyne-Beresford laughed, '...but an acquaintance of Lieutenant Wright's insisted that you stay here.'

Gwen peered out to see Kitty in the arms of a young woman of about her age. Both of them were jumping up and down and squealing, ignoring the stares of the passers-by. Thankfully they stopped before they garnered too much attention and Kitty dragged her friend over as Gwen got out of the autocar.

'Gwen! This is Nicole, remember me telling you about her?'

Gwen smiled fondly at Kitty's girlish behaviour, but then started. 'Nicole?' Her eyes shot to the young woman. She was tall, with dark hair and dark eyes, wearing a white sun dress, which showed off long, olive-skinned limbs. 'Nicole Tesla?'

The woman nodded. 'Guilty as charged! And you must be Gwen.' She stepped forwards and gave her an enthusiastic hug, which made the bones of Gwen's corset creak. 'I'm so looking forward to getting to know you! Kitty hasn't told me nearly enough about you!'

She gave Gwen a last crushing squeeze, then stepped back. 'You must be exhausted after such a long journey and then having to sit through those speeches.' She shook her head. 'So boring! I was listening on the radio and fell asleep two minutes after Senator Gould started speaking.' She stroked Kitty's arm. 'Yours was very good, though. Funny and to the point. Very refreshing. Very British. I almost couldn't recognise you!'

Kitty shrugged. 'I've been away a long time.'

'But you haven't changed a bit.' Nicole smiled at Kitty, her hand still on her arm. She stayed like that for a few seconds, but then suddenly laughed and spun in place. Insinuating herself between the two pilots, she wrapped an arm around each of them and pulled them towards the hotel door. 'Come on, let's grab a bite to eat, then I'll take you to your room.'

She spoke to Gascoyne-Beresford over her shoulder without stopping. 'You can have them back in a couple of hours, OK?'

The aide nodded. 'Very well, Miss Tesla, I will have the autocar sent back for them at four.' He looked at Gwen and Kitty. 'You'll be meeting the consul at the consulate before we go to your first engagement, a welcome dinner at the town hall. I recommend you get some rest; the mayor likes dancing and you're sure to be in demand.'

He smiled, raised his umbrella to them in salute, then got back into the autocar, which rejoined the traffic on the avenue.

An extremely quick electric elevator took them to the restaurant at the very top of the hotel. A waiter hurried over to them as soon as the doors opened and he greeted Nicole by name, then ushered them to a table up against the floor to ceiling windows that comprised one entire wall. Gwen walked straight past it, though; she was captivated by her first real view of the city. It was a spectacular view, akin to the one she had from an aircraft, but, rather than being fleeting as she flew by at hundreds of miles an hour, she actually had time to enjoy it.

Despite the impression she'd gotten from the undersea boat, not all of the buildings in New York were monstrosities of fifty storeys or more. In fact, most of the ones around the hotel, in the middle of the island, were shorter even than its twenty-five floors and didn't do much to block her view of the horizon. Things became rather more indistinct the further away they were, though, because there was a brown, smudgy haze over everything - further testament to the widespread usage of internal combustion engines.

The park was laid out beneath her and she had a bird's-eye view of the goings on at the airship landing field at its south end. Two of the largest airships she'd ever seen, beyond Bertha, of course, were securely tied down next to the terminal building, one of them disgorging a tide of passengers even as she watched. They would be the vessels that took passengers who preferred to travel by air, rather than use the excellent rail system that had driven the unification of the country, across the length and breadth of America. There were also four much smaller airships berthed to one side, against the perimeter fence, but they appeared to not have been used for a while and most likely they were privately owned.

Much as she liked airships - she owned one herself after all and planned to refurbish it with Kitty one day - she wasn't as interested in them as she was in other aircraft, and she soon lifted her gaze. The East River was only half a dozen blocks from Central Park and it was there, on Blackwell's Island, that Pellegrini Airport could be found. The airstrip took up most of the long, thin island and there was a steady stream of aircraft moving to and from its single runway. Thankfully, they were far more organised now than they had been earlier, during the undersea boat's arrival, but there was still such an eclectic mix of craft, with varying speeds and glide path requirements, that it must have been a headache for the air traffic controllers to keep them organised.

There were two other airstrips serving Manhattan, one to its north and one to the west, but Pellegrini was by far the busiest of the three. That was partly because it was the closest to some of the more upmarket areas of the city and therefore convenient for the well-off who could afford a private aircraft. The main reason, though, was that, despite all three of them being off the island and across rivers, it was the only one linked to the city by one of Nicola Tesla's inventions - an underground train that levitated on magnetic tracks. It was necessary to come by road from the other two, braving the traffic and crossing bridges, and the journey would often take longer than it would have done just to walk, whereas Tesla's train took only three minutes to get into the city, arriving at a station underneath the very hotel she was in. Pellegrini was so much in demand, actually, that they had started expanding the airport and were famously building an innovative three-storey hangar on the limited space of the island to accommodate more aircraft.

She squinted and pressed her face to the glass in an attempt to spot some sign of the construction work, curious as to how advanced it was and what it looked like, but that part of the airfield was obscured by a cloud of dust and fumes and she couldn't see much of anything.

'You'll have to excuse Gwen, she's been gawping at everything since we surfaced in the bay.'

'Eh? What?' Gwen turned to find Kitty and Nicole watching her from seats at the table. They already had drinks so she must have been staring out of windows for a while. 'Sorry!' She blushed and hurried to her chair, which a waiter was patiently holding out for her. 'Thank you.'

Nicole had everything organised and food arrived almost immediately. It was delicious and just what the pilots needed after being stuck in a tin can for over a week with only Royal Navy rations on offer.

Kitty and Nicole naturally dominated the conversation, catching up on what had happened to them in the years they'd last seen each other and Gwen mostly concentrated on her food, only interjecting every so often when she was asked to fill in details Kitty was missing. She stopped paying attention altogether when dessert came, though, and was so engrossed in a spectacular confection of caramel and chocolate that she didn't notice when her companions fell silent. The first thing she knew that something was going on was when her instincts told her that someone was approaching behind her. She twisted in her seat to check her six and found a spry old gentleman in a rather outmoded grey suit hobbling up to the table, supporting himself with a silver-topped cane.

Nicole leapt out of her seat and ran to embrace the man. 'Grampa! I didn't know you were in town!'

Kitty smiles as she stood and went around the table to do the same, but Gwen could only sit and stare.

The pictures in the history books always showed him as a young man, but, even though his face was more gaunt and his black hair and moustache had turned grey, it was undoubtedly Nikola Tesla standing three feet from her.

'Hello, Kitty, nice to see you again.'

'Hi, Mr Tesla! It's been too long.'

'Indeed it has.' The old man smiled warmly, then looked down at Gwen. 'Welcome back to my hotel, Miss Hawking.'

'Back?' Gwen frowned.

Tesla chuckled. 'I had the pleasure of playing host to you and your parents in twenty-two, but you were very young and I don't suppose you would recall. I remember *you* well, though. You made a great impression on me even then and, although it's not exactly my field, I have been following your career with interest.'

'Oh... Thank you.'

Gwen didn't know quite what else to say, but she was spared from any awkwardness by Nicole, who interrupted as soon as she could.

'Join us, Grampa? Please? It's been so long since I've seen you. I'm sure Kitty and Gwen won't mind.'

'Yes, please, sir, do.' Gwen said, finally recovering a modicum of the composure she'd lost in meeting one of her childhood heroes.

'Very well, I will, thank you.' Tesla smiled warmly and allowed Nicole to help him to a chair. 'But you must call me Niko, Miss Hawking.'

'It's Mrs Stone, Grampa. *Squadron Leader* Stone, actually.'

'Oh, I do apologise.'

Gwen waved away Tesla's apology, 'That's alright, you weren't to know, and I'd be honoured if you'd call me Gwen.'

'The honor would be mine, Gwen.' Tesla settled in his seat with a small sigh and accepted a small cup of coffee from the waiter who appeared at his elbow. 'I have a model of your Excalibur, by the way. A remarkable design. It's a shame the war got in the way of your career. However, while war may bring many things to a halt and set us back as human beings, it does have a habit of driving innovation, does it not?' He gave her a smile, tilting his head to one side in a curious fashion, like a bird, before turning to his granddaughter. 'Speaking of which, how is your project coming along, Nicole?'

'I've got it working. After a fashion anyway.'

'After a fashion?' Tesla grinned. 'Usually when someone says that it means it *doesn't* work.'

Nicole nodded earnestly. 'It does! Really! It's just, well, it only works under certain, rather specific circumstances.'

Tesla laughed gently. 'I've lost count of the number of times an invention of mine only worked "under certain specific circumstances" in its early days of development. Persevere; those circumstances will widen eventually, trust me.'

Nicole sighed. 'I'm not sure whether they will. I've tried everything. Are you sure you couldn't...?'

Tesla shook his head. 'You know how I feel about weapons.' He sipped his coffee, then looked at Kitty. 'But maybe your old lab partner could bring a new perspective.'

Kitty sat up in her seat. 'Are you still working on our cannon?'

Nicole nodded. 'With varying success.'

'I'm working on it too, but I had to stop because,' she shrugged, 'well, you know.'

'Did you get anywhere?' Nicole leaned forward eagerly.

'I...'

'Ladies, please!' Tesla held up his hands. 'Swap notes later!' He pointedly looked around the restaurant. While not even half of the tables were occupied, there were still quite a few people within earshot. 'This is neither the time nor the place.'

'Yes, Grampa.' Nicole slumped back in her chair, pouting.

Tesla leaned over and laid his hand on hers. 'When you've had your first breakthrough pilfered by unscrupulous men, you'll understand.' He gave her hand a pat. 'Perhaps you could show our guests around your lab?'

'Yes!' Nicole said excitedly, 'that would be fun!'

Kitty pulled her itinerary out of the tiny purse that came with her dress uniform and scanned it quickly. 'They haven't really left us very much time to ourselves...'

'I'm quite sure an opening will be found.' Tesla gave Kitty a knowing smile then looked at Gwen. 'I'm afraid I must be going, but Gwen, I'd like to speak privately with you some time, if I may?'

Gwen blinked, surprised. 'Of course.'

'Wonderful.' He lifted a hand and a waiter appeared behind him to pull his chair out and help him stand. 'Thank you for your hospitality and good luck with the mission!'

The old scientist hobbled away, collecting aides from a nearby table as he did.

Gwen watched him until the lift doors closed on him, then turned to smile at Kitty. 'Gosh!'

Kitty laughed. 'Gosh indeed!'

With dessert done and none of them wanting coffee, lunch was finished and, much as they would have loved to linger and simply chat while enjoying the view, there just wasn't the time.

Nicole took them one floor down to their room, an enormous suite with three bedrooms, each with its own bathroom, a lounge, a kitchen, and a terrace overlooking the park. It was far too much for them and they said as much, but Nicole just laughed, told them to enjoy themselves, winked, then left.

Their meagre luggage was waiting for them in the main bedroom, but they ignored it and went out onto the terrace.

They stood at the railing and looked out at the vibrant city.

London had been much like New York before the war, but the British capital had been made quiet and her people rendered fearful by the constant bombing. With the loss of Malta and Greece and the forces based in Gibraltar and Egypt under siege it didn't look like that was going to change any time soon, in fact it was only likely to get worse.

The only way things would ever go back to how they had been was if someone came to their rescue. Britain already had an ally in Muscovy, but they were beset by the Prussians and too busy defending themselves to help. America, on the other hand, had resources and manpower to spare and could easily relieve the pressure, giving Britain the breathing room she needed to hold on and perhaps recover enough to counter attack.

If they succeeded in their mission there was a chance that the shadow of war would fall over the American people as well. However, there was no guarantee that Prussia wouldn't reach its feelers out over the ocean once Europe was subdued anyway and by then America would be on its own.

It was clearly better for the whole world, therefore, if they came into the fight sooner rather than later.

If only they could be convinced of that.

It was a daunting task that the king had set for them and it had caused them quite a few sleepless nights on the journey, but now they were there it didn't seem so impossible; the reception they had received proved that they had support for their cause.

Gwen was still decidedly worried about how things were going to go, though, and the prospect of standing up in front of a crowd of women didn't do anything to relieve her unease. However, the mission was the last thing on Gwen's mind at that moment, instead, there was a burning question she needed to ask. She turned from the magnificent view and scowled at Kitty.

'So. About you and Nicole...'

Kitty chuckled. 'That didn't take you long.'

CHAPTER 2

After unpacking and freshening up, there was just enough time for a short lie down before reception rang to say that the consulate's autocar had arrived to pick them up. They got back into their dress uniforms as quickly as the awkward corsets and petticoats would allow them, made sure their hair was in place, grabbed their hats, then took the lift down to the ground floor.

Gascoyne-Beresford was waiting for them in the lobby and he smiled broadly as he led them out to the autocar idling outside the door. 'Good afternoon! I hope you managed to rest a bit, because we've got a long night ahead of us.'

Gwen waited until they were all settled in their seats before answering. 'Not much, but we're used to long hours.'

Kitty nodded. 'We thought it was more important to get some decent food down us for the first time in weeks.'

'Undersea boat food...' The aide shuddered exaggeratedly. 'I don't blame you! Well, you won't have to worry about your palates for the next week or two. In fact we have you going to so many breakfasts, brunches, luncheons, teas, suppers, dinners and soirees that I think you'll have to worry more about fitting in your cockpits when you get back.'

'Actually, I wanted to talk to you about that.' Kitty said. 'Is there any way you can find some time off for us in the next few days? A couple of hours would be enough at a pinch, but an afternoon would be best.'

The aide frowned. 'Your schedules were extremely hard to put together, it would be almost impossible to change anything without it all falling apart. Can't the sightseeing wait until you come back from Venezuela?'

Kitty shook her head. 'It's not sightseeing.'

'Although that would be quite nice...' Gwen put in hopefully.

Kitty grinned at her before turning back to the aide. 'Actually, Nicole invited us to her workshop and I'd really like to go, because...'

Gascoyne-Beresford sat forward excitedly, cutting her off before she could explain herself. 'You've been invited to her laboratory?' He rubbed his hands together in glee. 'We've been trying to get one of our, how shall I put it... our *special* people in there for ages, but this is so much better! You two are more than capable of evaluating what might be of use to us as you look around and that will save us a *whole* lot of bother. Your reports will be far more detailed, too.'

'You want us to report on Nicole Tesla's work?' asked Gwen with some distaste.

'Yes, of course! Hers *and* Tesla's if you can. Their labs are next to each other at the Wardenclyff compound, so see if you can get her to let you in there as well.'

Kitty shook her head. 'I don't think...'

Gascoyne-Beresford tutted and waggled his finger at them playfully, interrupting her again. 'Come now, there is no need to be like that. Either of you. You're not being asked to steal anything - it's not as if we'd be able to replicate any of their work after just a single look anyway - we just want to know what they have. If America comes into this war on our side then Tesla's inventions will likely come with her, but if the worst comes to the worst and America joins the Prussians, then we need to have an idea what we may have to deal with. And anyway, even if we were asking you to do something unseemly, I, personally, believe that it is the duty of everyone who wears the king's uniform to do *whatever* they can for their country. Don't you?' He turned his languid gaze on Gwen for a few seconds, then looked back at Kitty. 'The consul could always make it an order if that will make you more comfortable?'

As scientists themselves, the women had a natural dislike of anyone who would steal someone else's ideas, but that didn't mean they didn't see the necessity or know it was their duty to use the situation to the utmost advantage, so they each nodded.

'Jolly good! And it's not as if it will be spying, anyway, because you've been invited!' The aide gave them a brilliant smile, then flopped back in his seat and turned his head to gaze out of the window, letting them know that the conversation was at an end.

Gwen grimaced at Kitty, receiving a shrug in reply, but they said nothing and just held hands in silence for the rest of the short journey.

The British Consulate was four blocks to the east of Tesla's hotel and five to the south. It occupied the whole of the thirteenth floor of one of the taller buildings in the area, a rather uninspiring and nondescript block of grey stone and darkened windows.

As he led them along a blue carpeted corridor flanked by offices and lounges, Gascoyne-Beresford exchanged greetings with everyone they came across, even leaning through open doors to call out to people. From what Gwen saw once the aide had moved on she got the impression that he was well-liked, but wasn't taken very seriously, that he was actually seen as something of a clown. He either didn't notice or didn't mind and maintained his carefree attitude all the way down the exceedingly long corridor to a wooden door at the very end. He didn't knock or go in, though, but came to a halt and consulted a military-style chronograph on his left wrist.

'It'll just be one moment.'

Gwen smiled as the aide bobbed his head almost imperceptibly and moved his lips, silently counting down. She wondered if he, or more likely the consul, was one of those men and women who insisted on extreme punctuality in everything they did and glanced at her own chronograph, the Frobisher her parents had given her, but it was seventeen minutes past the hour so she figured it was unlikely.

Twenty seconds later, Gascoyne-Beresford pulled down his sleeve, straightened his jacket, then knocked and opened the door without waiting for an answer.

The room beyond was a sizeable office on the corner of the building. It had large windows on two sides, but the placement of the consulate only half-way up the skyscraper meant that the views were not quite as impressive as the ones from the hotel, being mostly blocked by the surrounding towers. Four white leather sofas were set up to the side, grouped around a low coffee table, but it was the enormous wooden desk, directly in front of the door, that dominated the space and drew the attention on entering. Behind it was a woman with a halo of grey hair, wearing a rather masculine suit jacket over a blue dress, who looked up as they came in.

'Afternoon, madam. The Misfit Squadron pilots to see you.'

'Impeccable timing as always, John,' the woman said, as she placed an empty tea cup on its saucer. She pushed it to one side then stood and came around the desk to meet the two pilots, a broad smile on her face.

'Squadron Leader Stone, Aviator Lieutenant Wright, may I present His Majesty's Consul to the city of New York, Lady Rosemary Cooper.'

'It's not often I get a hero in my office, let alone two. Welcome!' She shook hands with them, then gestured to the sofas. She waited for them to all sit down, the pilots opposite her and the aide to one side, before speaking again. 'Would you like tea? Anything to eat?'

'No, thank you,' Gwen replied after glancing at Kitty. 'We're being well taken care of at the hotel.'

'By Nicole Tesla.' Gascoyne-Beresford added, with a pointed look.

'Ah, yes.' The consul nodded. 'I was informed she was a, uh, friend of yours, Lieutenant Wright. Would you... that is to say... well, it's quite a delicate matter, but, uh, regarding Miss Tesla and her father... Would you...'

Cooper hesitated, embarrassed in a very British way and obviously just as uncomfortable as the pilots had been with the subject at hand, but feeling obliged to ask nonetheless.

Thankfully, Gascoyne-Beresford interrupted, saving her having to do so. 'Miss Tesla has invited Squadron Leader Stone and Aviator Lieutenant Wright to her laboratory. I have already filled them in on the importance of keeping their eyes and ears open during the visit.'

'Oh? Has she? How marvellous!' Cooper's eyes shone. 'I don't know if John told you, but we've been trying to get a look into the Wardenclyff facility for years.'

Kitty nodded. 'He did say something to that effect, ma'am.'

'Well, it's true.' Cooper said, then went on hurriedly. 'Not that we want to steal anything. We just want to know what's there. For our own peace of mind.'

'He said something to that effect too, ma'am.'

'Good. Good.'

'Mr Tesla has also asked to speak to me privately while we're there.' Gwen added.

Gascoyne-Beresford frowned at her. 'You didn't tell me that.'

Gwen shrugged. 'I didn't think it was important. Apparently he played host to my parents when they were here for a conference in 1922, so he may just want to catch up on what they've been doing since, or feels like he should show hospitality to the daughter of some old friends.'

'Maybe. But maybe not.' The consul pursed her lips thoughtfully. 'We're fairly sure that Tesla is sympathetic to our cause and that he would like the Americans to join the war against the Prussians, but he's never said it outright, perhaps because he famously doesn't trust politicians and wouldn't speak to people John and I. He might have decided to say something to you, though.'

'Tesla is a very popular man because of his charity work and how he has used his inventions to improve the country.' Gascoyne-Beresford said. 'His "Generator Foundation", for example, provides free electricity to millions of impoverished people all over the country. So, if he does say something of the sort to you and you can persuade him to also make a public statement, it could sway a lot of people...'

'A lot of voters,' Cooper interjected.

The aide nodded in agreement. 'Quite right, ma'am. It could sway a lot of *voters* to our side and then the American politicians would have to take notice.'

'Maybe that's too much to hope for,' the consul said, 'it would cause quite a lot of trouble for him, lose him a lot of sales. You know how Americans are with only buying from people they like' She frowned thoughtfully. 'He could want to give you something, though. An invention of some description. That way he could help us without being seen to take sides.'

Gwen shrugged. 'Or, as I said, he might just want to have a chat.'

Cooper laughed. 'That is a possibility, of course. However, in my experience, someone like Tesla never simply "wants to chat", but I suppose we will find out what he really wants in due course. John, can you make time for them to...?'

'Already done, ma'am, I've cleared their schedule for Friday afternoon.'

'The day after tomorrow? That doesn't give us time to brief them on what to look for.'

'There is no need for a particularly exhaustive brief, ma'am; they're not just pilots, they're scientists as well. They will be able to separate the wheat from the chaff.'

'Marvellous! Well, then, please don't let me keep you; there's a lot to do before we head off to the mayor's shindig. I will leave you in John's capable hands.' Cooper stood and offered her hand again, then turned away and went back to her desk as Gascoyne-Beresford ushered them from the room.

A few doors down the hall was a meeting room with a large wooden table and a dozen chairs around it. A couple of cheval glasses had been placed against the wall to one side and there were several clothes racks filled with blue dresses on either side of them.

Gascoyne-Beresford left them there, in the care of three women, who had been sipping tea at the table while they waited. The two youngest, barely more than teenagers, stood by, watching attentively, as the third, a woman in her forties wearing an outfit similar to Cooper's, looked them up and down, tutting at their dress uniforms. 'So 1890's.'

Gwen raised an eyebrow. 'Maybe that's because they were designed in 1892?'

The woman huffed. 'It shows, dear. It shows.' She idly ran a finger along the dresses hanging from one of the racks while she studied Gwen. 'The trouble with women's military uniforms is that they are military uniforms and the military has been dominated by men for far too long. They were invariably designed by men and either make no concession to the female anatomy or, if they do, are so feminine that they lose any pretence at being martial.' She pulled one of the dresses out slightly, but then pushed it back with a frown. 'My name's Vera, by the way, Vera Huppe, and Georgey has charged me with creating something special for your upcoming social engagements. Something that allows you to be feminine, while at the same time leaving no doubt that you are warriors.' She waved a hand dismissively at their uniforms. 'Unlike those monstrosities, which, honestly, should have been consigned to a museum decades ago.'

'Why not just daub us with woad and be done with it?' The American woman's obvious disdain of their traditional uniforms, designed at the time with the latest Victorian fashions in mind, was really rubbing Gwen up the wrong way and the words came out before she had a chance to think about them.

The woman didn't seem offended, though, and just shrugged. 'I did suggest that to Georgey, but he rightly pointed out that you might cause too many heart attacks when you address the two houses.'

Gwen glanced at Kitty, expecting her to be at least a little offended, but the American was grinning. Frowning, she turned back to the woman just in time to have a dress shoved into her hands.

'Here. Try this on.'

The woman didn't wait for an answer, but immediately switched her attention to Kitty, whose smile only got wider.

'Hi, Auntie Vera.'

Gwen glared at her friend, but the American only winked before folding the woman in a hug.

'Kitty, dearest! You're looking good.' The woman smiled for the first time, but it disappeared immediately as she pulled back and eyed Kitty critically. 'The measurements they gave me are wrong. Have you put on weight?'

'I was injured a while back and was still recovering when they measured me in London.'

'Ah.' The woman nodded, then called over her shoulder to her assistants without even glancing at them, 'two, half, one and a half. It'll only take the girls a few minutes to adjust your dresses and in the meantime you can fill me in on what you've been doing.' She took Kitty by the arm and pulled her over to a couple of chairs at the table.

Gwen watched them sit and start talking, laughing gently together. 'I guess I'll get changed, then,' she muttered under her breath.

A folding screen had been set up in the corner of the room and she went to it. She hung her dress over it, then stepped back to get a better look at it.

'Oh.'

All of the outfits on the racks were in RAC blue and she could imagine that Huppe had gnashed her teeth in frustration at a limitation that had undoubtedly been imposed on her by the king. However, apart from that one requirement, it seemed that she had been given free rein and the garment was like no uniform she had ever seen.

It was understandable that the king wanted his representatives to have a new dress uniform to wear to their engagements in America. The corsets and petticoats of the old one were terribly old-fashioned, but, more than that, they were impractical, coming as they did from an age where a woman wasn't expected to do anything even remotely physical - not only were the petticoats so voluminous that they made it extremely hard for a man to get close enough to dance properly, but, thanks to the corsets, the woman would be passing out from oxygen starvation after only a few minutes if one did succeed in doing so.

Huppe had, at least with this particular dress, gone to the other extreme, though. It wasn't tight or restricting and there was nothing of volume to it, however, that was largely because the material could at best have been described as *diaphanous* and at worst *transparent*.

One of the young women left off adjusting Kitty's dresses and came over to help her, but she barely needed the assistance as the garment slipped over her head and fell into place with ease.

Gwen looked at herself in the mirror and blushed. Apart from a few opaque panels covering her most intimate parts her entire body was on display, including a large part of her comfortable, but rather well-worn and faded, underpants.

'Lovely!' Huppe hurried over. She pulled the shoulders of the dress and fluffed it out.

'It's not bad.' Gwen couldn't help but agree that it was rather fetching, but it seemed more like a nightie than a ball gown. It certainly wasn't a uniform. 'It's not really very martial, though, is it? And I'm not sure about going out in public like this...' she twisted and shuddered at how much of her rear could be glimpsed through the material.

'Nonsense! It's modelled after the classic sketches of Britannia. You couldn't get much more martial than that! And you look spectacular!'

'You really do.' Kitty came into view behind Gwen in the mirror and made a point of looking her up and down hungrily.

'And besides,' Huppe continued, 'the armour will leave no room for doubt.'

Before Gwen could even think about asking whether the woman was joking, the second assistant appeared behind her and reached up to hang something over her head.

Gwen flinched and closed her eyes as whatever it was passed inches in front of her face, but opened them again when a weight settled over her shoulders and gaped at the sight in the mirror.

The dress itself might have been soft and flowing, but the addition of a shining gold breastplate and shoulder guards made her appearance far more martial. However, if the outfit had been rather suggestive before, now it was overtly sexual, with the breastplate doing as much as a corset ever had to accentuate her "assets".

Kitty was now staring at her open mouthed, almost panting, and Gwen had to admit that she did look rather impressive, even if she did want to cover herself with a shawl. She couldn't help but feel completely overdressed and slightly comical, though, like an actor in a patriotic photograph or play.

'No, she can't wear that,' said Huppe, waving away the assistant who was struggling to bring over a helmet, shield and eight-foot long trident.

'Why...' Kitty coughed as her voice hitched in her throat. 'Why not?'

Huppe grinned at her. 'Look at yourself in the mirror, dearest - that's why not. We want her to be taken seriously as a woman and a warrior, not seen simply as something to be taken to bed and ravaged.'

'Aw...' Kitty returned the grin. 'Can we keep it, though?'

Huppe laughed. 'Of course, my dear! But wait until you see what else I have before you burden yourself with this one.'

'Are you saying that there's more that look...' Gwen said, gesturing at her chest, which seemed to stick out half a mile, 'like this?'

Huppe nodded. 'There are a few that are designed to bring out the best in you, so to speak.' She sighed regretfully. 'But maybe we can skip those.'

'Not on your life!' said Kitty, laughing at Gwen's horrified look.

'*That's* the girl who used to model for me! Willing to try anything, no matter how carried away I got!' Huppe turned to the clothing rack, rubbing her hands together. 'Right, next!'

Over the next hour Gwen and Kitty tried on more than a dozen concoctions, including a couple more that incorporated pieces of armour in some way, one made up entirely of feathers and incorporating extendable wings, and one that was similar to a male dress uniform, with long jackets over fitted waistcoats and extremely tight breeches, but with the addition of feminine touches like blouses and ruffles.

Gwen was beginning to despair of there being anything that she wouldn't be ashamed of wearing in public when Huppe brought a halt to the proceedings and put a hand on her arm.

'Don't worry, dear, those were just me having a bit of fun at Georgey's expense. I'll probably end up selling a few to Broadway shows and the like, but they're not for wearing out. I do however have one last one that is a little more... *conventional.*'

Gwen dreaded what the woman's idea of conventional was going to be so she gave her a weak smile and resignedly put on the blue tights and white silk shirt an assistant brought. She didn't even glance at the jacket she was helped into and it was only when she went and looked into the mirror that she really took any notice of what she was wearing.

'Gosh!'

This outfit might well have been more conventional than the other ones, but that didn't make it anything less striking and Gwen couldn't resist reaching up to stroke the wide lapels of the long leather jacket.

'I knew you would like it.' Huppe said.

'Saving the best for last, Auntie?' asked Kitty.

'Of course, dear!'

'You know you could have saved a lot of time if you'd just brought this out first.'

'Where would the fun be in that?'

Gwen barely heard the two bickering good-naturedly, like the old friends they were; she was too busy marvelling at what she was wearing. Made of a soft and supple leather that had been dyed RAC blue, the jacket was surprisingly light, even though it fell to her ankles. It was cut like a gown, with a fairly low bodice and a tight waist, which gave the impression she was wearing a corset, without her actually having to wear one, but the silk shirt meant that she was showing far less than she had with any of the other outfits. While most of the things that Huppe had shown them had conceivably been acceptable as a dress uniform or as evening wear, none of them had worked as both, but this was elegant enough to go to a ball in, even though it was made of leather, while still managing to be something that wouldn't look out of place on a parade ground. It was also the first one that she felt she would be comfortable wearing.

She twisted back and forth, admiring herself, marvelling at how the skirts of the jacket flared as if it were a ball gown and was surprised to find that her movement was completely unrestricted, despite how tightly fitting it was.

She smiled as Kitty came up beside her.

'I think we've found a winner, don't you?' Kitty said, looking Gwen up and down, open admiration in her expression.

Gwen nodded. 'I do. I really do.'

She looked down, wanting to investigate a few oddities she'd noticed in the jacket, but was prevented from doing so when the American grabbed hold of her and spun her into her arms. She began to close her eyes, expecting, and hoping for, a kiss, but squealed and scrabbled to hold on when she started propelling her across the floor, humming a waltz.

'Come on, darling! We have to test it fully!' The waltz became something far more energetic as Kitty spun Gwen and she almost tripped over herself again before finding the new rhythm. She was really starting to enjoy herself, getting caught up in the moment and in Kitty's enthusiasm, but when she noticed Huppe and her two assistants watching them she suddenly became self-conscious. She stumbled and stalled, losing the beat, and came to a halt.

The three women clapped and Kitty laughed as Gwen blushed, smoothing down skirts that didn't need smoothing.

'This is so... so...'

'Perfect.' Kitty finished Gwen's thought as Huppe came over and inspected them.

'I'm glad you like it,' the woman said, 'but they're not complete yet.' She gestured to a stack of boxes on a table against the wall. 'You need accessories.'

She led them to the table and started to pull items out of the boxes. 'Try these on first.'

She handed a pair of long black boots to each of the pilots, then leaned back against the table to wait.

Gwen took hers and started to put them on, but then stopped and took a closer look. 'These are flight boots.'

'Uh huh,' Huppe said. 'They've got a bit of a heel for the evening, but not much, so they can double as flight boots.'

Gwen frowned. 'But why? What's the point if...? Oh!'

Huppe laughed. 'I was wondering how long it would take one of you to work it out.'

It was Kitty's turn to frown. 'Work out what?'

Gwen smiled at her, but instead of answering she began making adjustments to her clothing. The wide lapels were the most obvious place to start and they closed across her chest, clipping into place on the hidden fasteners she'd noticed when holding Kitty during the dance. The skirts were a bit more complicated and it took a few seconds for her to figure out how they worked, but then it was a matter of only a few seconds to split them down the front and back, then wrap a pair of concealed leather panels around her legs and secure them snugly in place. She straightened up when she'd finished and held her arms out, presenting herself to Kitty. 'That our new dress uniforms are also flight suits.'

'Gosh!' Kitty said, winking at her.

Gwen smiled, but then immediately turned back to Huppe. 'What other little secrets is this hiding?'

Huppe raised an eyebrow. 'What makes you think there's anything else?'

'Because you don't strike me as being someone who does things by half measures.'

'How right you are, dear.' Huppe gave Gwen a wink, then pointed at her legs. 'First off, there are watertight compartments in the trousers. You can fill them with any liquid that's handy, even wine or whisky if that's all you've got,' she waved her hand vaguely, 'you know, for the gravity stuff.'

'Yes, we know.' Kitty said, looking up from fiddling with her own trousers.

Huppe smiled at her. 'Just make sure you rinse them out afterwards with some distilled water, otherwise they'll get damaged or start smelling and people might think you're drunk all the time.'

Gwen and Kitty laughed and Huppe joined in briefly before going back to business. There were two hat boxes on the table and she pulled top hats from them. 'Here. What do you think of these, then, clever clogs?'

Gwen turned hers over in her hands. It appeared like an ordinary dress uniform hat, identical to the ones they already had, however...

'It's too heavy. Why is that?' Kitty asked, putting her hat on her head. 'This won't work as a flight helmet.'

'Of course it won't,' Gwen said, meeting Huppe's eyes. 'The helmet's inside, isn't it?'

'In the lining. Along with the gloves.'

Gwen felt around the satin lining until she found the hooks attaching it to the hat and carefully undid them, revealing a small wooden compartment which hinged open smoothly. Inside were a pair of fur-lined leather flight gloves and a leather helmet, both of which matched the jacket. There was also a small felt bag.

'Careful does it,' warned Huppe, as Gwen tugged at the bag, 'you don't want to damage the lenses.'

'Lenses?' Gwen said. 'This bag isn't nearly big enough to hold... oh!'

Most lens arrays were large, heavy, unwieldy contraptions with up to a dozen lenses held together with metal mountings. They were complicated, delicate and the best ones were horribly expensive. However, there were no lenses on the goggles in the bag, instead there was only a thin metal tube attached to each side.

'Let me show you how they work.' Huppe took the goggles from Gwen and showed her the tube. 'These are clockwork. You wind them up before flying.' The end of the tube clicked gently as she twisted it. 'I won't wind them fully, I'll just give them half a turn so that you can try them. Here, put them on.'

Gwen took them and turned them back and forth. 'Where's the wire? How do I plug them in?'

'There's no wire.' Huppe said with a grin.

Gwen shared a look with Kitty, who just shrugged and fiddled with her own goggles.

Huppe turned a dial on the back of one of the gloves before handing them over. 'Now these.'

Gwen slipped them on and flexed her fingers experimentally while she inspected them a bit closer. The dial was part of a thin box on the back of the left one, but it was only really a switch with two settings - on and off. Apart from that there were no other knobs, buttons, or wheels to be found, which was puzzling, because it made no sense to have the controls for the lenses anywhere else.

'Alright, go look out the window.'

One of the assistants raised the blind on one of the windows and Kitty and Gwen went to stand in front of it.

'Now what?' Kitty asked, craning her head to look down at the people and vehicles on the street.

'Now touch your ring finger to your thumb.'

'Wow!'

'What? What?' Gwen asked, looking down at her hand. 'Mine's not doing anything.'

'Left hand, dear.'

'Oh, alright. It's just I usually have the controls for my lenses on my right... Gosh!'

The buildings over the other side of the street shot towards her and she found herself looking through a window at a man picking his nose as he read a newspaper at his desk. She hurriedly lifted her eyes skywards, seeking out an aircraft. There were dozens to choose from in the gaps between the buildings and she found one immediately and touched her thumb to her finger again to bring it closer. She misjudged her aim slightly and the aircraft, a small biplane, disappeared from her view. Correctly guessing that she had to touch her thumb to her little finger to zoom out she tried again, but lost sight of the aircraft as she retracted her vision too much.

'This is going to take a bit of getting used to.'

'I'm told you can adjust the sensitivity of the controls.' Huppe said. 'I was given a manual,' she looked around the room, 'but I have no idea where it is. I'll have it sent to you when I find it.'

'Thank you.' Gwen took the goggles off carefully and held them up to the light. Now that she knew what she was looking for, she could see the lenses lying against the protective glass. When she pressed her fingers together, they were moved out and back by a mechanism in the tubes on the sides. 'These must be expensive!'

'They are.' Huppe nodded. 'But they were the most portable option and, anyway, Georgey is paying.'

'And how are they controlled without wires?'

'It's one of Tesla's inventions, isn't it?' said Kitty.

'I think so.' Huppe said.

'I knew he was working on the wireless transmission of electrical energy, but I never thought it would work, or be capable of doing something so delicate. I wonder how they make sure the image is always in focus.'

Huppe laughed. 'Don't look at me, I just had them made to measure for you. I can give you the name of the manufacturer if you want; maybe they'll be able to explain it.'

'Actually, I'd quite like to figure it out myself.'

Gwen sighed. 'Just make sure you know how to put them back together again afterwards.'

'One time!' Kitty protested. 'One time I took apart that thingamajig in your workshop and didn't know how to put it back together!' She pouted. 'How was I to know it had acid in it and was going to melt a hole in your floor? As if anyone would leave something that dangerous just sitting around for anyone to play with?'

'Yes. Anyway...' Gwen shook her head, then smiled at Huppe. 'Thank you, this is truly wonderful.'

'You're welcome, dear.' Huppe smiled back, but then a pained look crossed her face and she turned to Kitty. She ran a hand down the American's arm as she spoke, not meeting her eyes. 'You know, I made this as soon as I heard you'd run off to Spain. I wanted you to be able to enjoy every minute of spare time you could, at a party or whatever, while still be ready to fly at a moment's notice and fight to the best of your abilities. When that went bad I thought you would never make it back to wear it.'

'Well, I'm here to wear it now, and I'll be wearing it a lot, if our schedule for the next few weeks is anything to go by. I have a feeling it's going to be very useful.'

'I'm glad.' Huppe smiled sadly and looked away quickly. 'As you said before, the hat is quite heavy with the gloves and helmet inside, but the box comes out and can be left behind if you know you're not flying.' She took a couple of small boxes from an assistant and handed one each to Gwen and Kitty. 'The uniform also comes with a white silk scarf, which I know you will have a use for in the air, and some white dress gloves.'

She paused and looked the women up and down with a critical eye. 'Perfect, I couldn't ask for a better advertisement for my work.'

Kitty frowned. 'Are things not going so well, then, auntie?'

Huppe shrugged. 'The war might not have reached us yet, but people are already feeling the effects and there isn't much call for new designs at the moment.'

'Well, we'll make sure that anyone who asks knows who we're wearing.'

'Thank you, dearest!' Huppe looked up as the door opened a crack and Gascoyne-Beresford poked his head around it.

'Is it safe to come in?' the aide asked.

'It's a bit late for that, isn't it?' Huppe said scornfully. 'You would have already caught an eyeful if it wasn't.'

Gascoyne-Beresford grinned at her, unabashed. 'I wouldn't have, because I've been eavesdropping.' He walked into the room, nodding appreciatively at the two pilots. 'Yes, that's much better. The way you looked was fine for mess dinners, I'm sure, but the Americans would have thought you extremely old-fashioned and unfashionable and dismissed you at first sight. They're going to eat this up, though, and I wouldn't be surprised if you started a few trends, either.'

'I'm *so* glad you approve.' Huppe said, rolling her eyes.

The aide ignored her and gestured at the door. 'This took far longer than it should have done and we only have twenty minutes until the reception starts. That's not enough time to brief you here, so we'll do it in the autocar. Leave your old uniforms, they'll be packaged up and sent to the hotel.'

Gwen and Kitty thanked the designer and her assistants, Kitty promising to have lunch with her aunt at the earliest opportunity, then followed Gascoyne-Beresford back towards the entrance of the consulate. He didn't poke his head into any of the offices as they went past, like he had when they had arrived, but he still had a word for every person they came across, many of whom gave the pilots admiring looks.

The autocar was waiting for them in front of the building and it pulled away as soon as the three of them were seated.

'Is the consul not coming?' Kitty asked, turning to peer out the back window at the pavement in front of the building, as if expecting the woman to come running out, waving for them to stop.

'She's already gone in her own autocar.' The aide said. 'As guests of honour you have to arrive last, so she has to get there before us or go unannounced. Now, if you don't mind, I have quite a few things to brief you about and not much time in which to do it.' He pulled a sheet of paper from his inside pocket and unfolded it, revealing a page of typed writing topped by a crest that Gwen didn't recognise. 'The names of your escorts for tonight are Estuardo Barton and...'

'Sorry?' Gwen interrupted. 'Our *escorts*? But Kitty and I are...'

She hesitated, glancing at Kitty, but the American just grinned.

'I'm pretty sure that Mr Gascoyne-Beresford is aware of the fact that we are in a relationship,' she raised an eyebrow at the aide, who nodded, 'however, we need male escorts. It's just how it's done, at least in formal occasions like this, which will be very public. There's no reason we can't dump them quickly, though; that's almost expected.'

Gascoyne-Beresford laughed. 'By all means "dump" them if you wish; once you've been announced their purpose will have been fulfilled. However, please bear in mind that they are precisely the kind of people we need to convince that they should be on our side. A dance won't kill you.'

'You obviously haven't seen Gwen dance.'

Gwen was about to retort, but Gascoyne-Beresford's impatient look silenced her and instead she settled for giving Kitty a swift jab in the side under cover of her jacket.

'As I was saying, Estuardo Barton, the son of an Ecuadorian oil tycoon, will be Miss Wright's escort, while Miss Stone will be escorted by Francis Edgerton, who...' he paused, his eyes opening in surprise as he read the page, 'who doesn't seem to be anybody special actually...' He frowned and turned the paper over then back again, searching for something that evidently wasn't there. Eventually he shook his head and went on. 'The American War Department insisted on choosing the escorts for us, instead of letting us do it, which is understandable really. They did promise two of their best and brightest, though, men from good families, so I'm not sure why...' still frowning, he trailed off as something on the page caught his attention and he went silent as he read. However, after a few seconds he shook his head again, then folded the page. He tucked it back into his pocket before smiling at them. 'I do apologise; we were only sent this information half an hour ago and I haven't had a chance to review it properly. Well, while the young men in question might not be exactly what we wanted, they are at least your age and pilots, or "flyers" as they insist on calling them - Edgerton is a captain in their land-based "Air Division", while Barton is a lieutenant in their "Naval Air Section". I'm given to believe those ranks are equivalent to each other, but I'm not sure if that's true or not. Whatever the case, you outrank them by quite a margin, so there won't be any awkwardness for you there. Furthermore, the Americans have said that they will be treating you both as foreign dignitaries at this kind of gathering throughout your visit. That will give you a higher rank than you really hold, which means that, once you're inside the residence and hats have come off, you won't have to worry about having to do all that silly stuff, like saluting or waiting for more senior officers to speak first.'

'So, we already know we're expected to dance and make nice,' said Kitty. 'What about a speech? Because you haven't given me anything for tonight.'

'And I don't think you want her blathering on like she usually does in these kinds of situations,' added Gwen, receiving a jab in reply from Kitty.

'You'll have to respond to the mayor's toast to the king with the standard "to the United Federation of American States and her people", but apart from that you won't be making any speeches, you'll just be making conversation. Keep it informal, please - you'll have plenty of chances to give reasons why America should do the right thing in the coming days, when you address the senate and such. Tonight is your chance to show that you are normal people, that you're trustworthy and worth listening to. If someone asks your opinion on the war and America's involvement, then by all means give it, but don't go out of your way to proselytise. Understood?'

The pilots nodded and he grinned cheerfully. 'Try to enjoy yourselves! But remember that you have things to do tomorrow, so don't drink yourselves into a stupor, even though the Americans probably will.'

The autocar slowed to turn into a long semi-circular driveway and came to a halt in front of a white marble colonnade leading to a pair of huge black doors.

Gascoyne-Beresford peered out and nodded in satisfaction. 'Here we are. Remember - best behaviour!'

'Yes, mother.'

The aide gave Kitty a scathing look, but said nothing as the door to the autocar was opened by a man in black livery. 'Off you go, then.'

'You're not coming with us?' asked Gwen.

'Of course not; I have to slink in the tradesman's entrance. I'll see you inside.'

Gwen got out, but didn't immediately follow Kitty towards the door. Instead, once the autocar had pulled away, she stepped out into the driveway and turned in place to take in the building and its surroundings.

In a city that seemed to be filled with nothing but skyscrapers she had expected the mayor's residence to be in yet another, but the sight of what could only be described as a palace was shocking. Shining white in the late afternoon sun, not only was it the only building she'd seen so far in the city that was wider than it was tall, but it looked like it was built from marble, rather than the ever present stone, metal and glass.

'When they were trying to decide where the capital of the United Federation would be, some of the richest people in the city got together to build this in an attempt to sway the vote. It was the first and only time the rich and powerful in this city set aside their differences and made something beautiful, instead of just competing to see who could place a girder the highest.'

The voice came from behind Gwen. It was male and unmistakably American and she had no doubt it would be that of her escort for the night. She turned to face the man, prepared to smile and be nice, but was rocked back in shock when she saw him.

The young man was gazing up at the building as he spoke, leaning back slightly with his hands in his pockets, so he didn't notice her reaction and kept speaking. 'This was supposed to house the entire government in one place, like your British Parliament. It has chambers for senate and congress, offices for everyone, several kitchens, dozens of bathrooms, and two hundred bedrooms for in case a debate goes on too long. This wing would have been the presidential residence, but now it's the mayor's.'

Gwen could barely hear him over the roaring in her ears as every dark feeling she'd had in the past couple of years came flying back all at once.

The round face. The dark blond hair peeking out from under the green cap. The nose that was slightly too large. The ears that stuck out just a bit too far. Somehow all the flaws came together to make something that was extremely attractive and very familiar...

'Richard?'

She barely managed to gasp the word out, but the man still heard her and paused in his monologue. He straightened up, taking his hands out of his pockets, and smiled at her. 'Uh, no, ma'am. The name's Edgerton. Captain Francis Edgerton. At your service.'

He sketched her a lazy salute, which she returned automatically while still staring at him.

'Everything alright, ma'am?'

'Sorry?' Gwen blinked and forced herself to smile. 'Oh, yes, everything is fine, thank you.' Over the man's shoulder she saw Kitty abandoning a young man in a blindingly white uniform at the door and coming towards them, her concern plain to see. 'Uh, would you give me a moment, please?'

'Of course.' The man nodded and retreated to the door to join his companion.

Gwen watched him go. Even the way he walked - loose-limbed and slovenly and distinctly unmilitarily - was reminiscent of Richard.

She shuddered.

'Gwen? What's wrong?' Kitty scowled at Edgerton's back. 'Did he say something to you?'

'No, he didn't say anything, it's... he's...'

'He's what?' Kitty grinned. 'Is he a past lover?'

Gwen looked up at her, startled. 'What made you say that?'

Kitty blinked. 'Nothing. I just thought it would be funny and lighten the mood. Why? Is he?'

'No. But...' Gwen bit her lip and stared at Edgerton. He was talking and laughing with the other pilot, a rather short, dark-haired man. Neither they nor the two black liveried men flanking the door were paying attention to the two women, but she still leaned in to Kitty and spoke quietly. 'My escort, Edgerton, he... he looks a heck of a lot like Richard.'

Kitty snapped her fingers. 'I *thought* he looked a bit familiar! It's not like I didn't see that picture you had in your cockpit enough times.' She peered at Edgerton, narrowing her eyes and tilting her head to the side. 'He *does* look pretty much like Richard, doesn't he? I should have noticed.' She grimaced suddenly and turned back to the Americans, lowering her voice to a hiss. '*Damn it.*'

'What?'

'You know what this means, right?'

Gwen shook her head. 'No, what?'

'The top brass in the military want us to fail.'

'What? How do you know?'

'Because they deliberately chose someone who looks like your dead husband in an attempt to unsettle you and ruin this night for us.' She shook her head. 'They must be desperate to resort to such a childish tactic.'

'Well, childish or not, it worked.'

Kitty grinned. 'I can see that.'

'Maybe I should go back to the hotel. I don't want to spoil things.'

The American stepped in front of Gwen, blocking her view of Edgerton. 'Hey! Look at me.'

Gwen turned her head up to meet Kitty's eyes.

'That's better. Now, if you don't want to spoil things then you're going to have to buck yourself up.'

'I don't want to spoil things.' Gwen said distractedly, craning her neck to see over Kitty's shoulder.

Kitty rolled her eyes. She grabbed the rim of Gwen's top hat and pulled her head around to face her, then leant forwards and fixed her eyes with her own. 'No matter how much he looks like Richard you *know* he isn't Richard. Now, come on. A couple of dances with this guy to show the idiots in charge you can't be shaken up so easily, then we'll ditch them and have some fun.'

Gwen met Kitty's gaze for a moment, then nodded. 'Alright. But if I can't do this I'll say I'm not feeling well and get Gascoyne- Beresford to take me back to the hotel.'

'That's fair enough.' Kitty straightened Gwen's hat, then leaned forwards and gave her a swift peck on the lips. 'Right, then. Time to face the music.'

She grabbed Gwen's hand and pulled her towards the waiting "flyers". 'You know, I have a cousin who looks a bit like me. I *really* hope you don't get confused when I take you to meet my family and fall in love with her.'

CHAPTER 3

The mayor's reception began like most such formal events did, with the guest of honour being announced and the national anthem of that guest being played. It wasn't the first formal reception Gwen had gone to - she had attended a few at Buckingham Palace during her time as a Misfit, as well as various around the world while travelling with her parents - but it was her first time as the guest of honour and that made it a very different experience.

As the British national anthem played, she stood rigidly to attention at the top of a short flight of stairs leading down to the reception room and couldn't help thinking back to the times, quite a few of them, when the guest of honour had been someone she, or others around her, had thought unworthy - like when the War Minister had been the guest of honour at one of the king's receptions, shortly before she and Kitty had left for America. It was the last time the surviving Misfits had been together and they had stood at the back, making snide comments the entire time he had been presented. Staring over their heads as she was, she couldn't see the people below, but she knew that their eyes were on her and couldn't help wondering how many of them were making those kinds of comments, or thinking similar thoughts. Or worse, how many of them were cursing her for bringing the war to their doorsteps and for trying to lure their young men to their deaths.

Thankfully, since Kitty was wearing the king's uniform the Americans only had to play one national anthem, so the time she had to remain on display wasn't very long. That was only the beginning of her discomfort, though, because, after the mayor had greeted her formally, there was the line up.

A line up was done so that the extremely important guest of honour could meet any other guests who were considered worthy of being known and acknowledged. In this case that included four senators, two ambassadors, the governor, several members of congress and half a dozen men and women whose wealth far eclipsed that of her parents - any one of whom she felt would be more worthy of walking the line than her.

If before she'd been feeling self-conscious, especially in her new dress uniform, now she felt like a fraud, pretending to be more than she was - a simple pilot.

The embarrassment didn't end there, either, because Mayor Winston took Gwen's arm as soon as the line up was finished and steered her around the room, introducing her to all and sundry as the ace pilot who had pretty much single-handedly won the battle over Britain of 1940 and would win the war if given the chance and enough American support.

Kitty followed behind throughout, all but ignored. Because Gwen was nominally the leader of the expedition the spotlight was on her for the evening, while Kitty was relegated to being little more than a novelty - an American in a British uniform - and she spent the whole time smirking at Gwen's discomfort, while chatting with Barton and Edgerton.

Eventually, though, not nearly soon enough for Gwen, it was time for the procession into the dining room for the banquet. The mayor, as host, would lead with his wife and Gwen would follow immediately after. It was precisely for this part of the evening that the escorts had been provided and under any other circumstances Gwen would be fine, she had after all been escorted in to dinner by many strangers over the years, but when Edgerton stepped forward and offered her his arm she found herself recoiling from him. She managed to stop herself before she made too much of a scene, though, and closed her eyes and took a deep breath.

He's not Richard. He's not Richard. A few repetitions of the mantra had her feeling almost normal again and she sighed inwardly. *This is like the plot to some bloody awful flyvie. Probably starring Hans Gruber.*

'Sorry?'

Gwen opened her eyes and looked at Edgerton, who smiled.

'Did you say something, ma'am?'

'What? Oh!' Gwen blushed, realising she must have said the last bit aloud. 'No, nothing.'

She forced herself to take his arm, but then started when a hand came down on her shoulder and spun around to find Kitty grinning at her.

'Hey! Move along there, wouldya? I'm hungry!'

Kitty pushed Gwen and she turned and staggered after the mayor, who was five yards away already and completely oblivious to the fact that nobody was following him.

Edgerton was caught by surprise and almost lost his grip on his arm as he stumbled, his dress shoes slipping on the polished marble floor of the corridor. He recovered quickly, demonstrating an agility that Richard had never had, and when he gave her a sheepish laugh, Gwen finally had a chance to get a proper look at him and found that wasn't the only way he differed from Richard. While some of the man's features certainly were similar to Richard's and as a whole he did indeed resemble her dead husband, that impression fell apart under closer inspection - the eyes were just a little too far apart, their blue more than a few shades too light, the lips were too thick and had a sarcastic twist to them that Richard's certainly hadn't had and he was a good two inches shorter. The last straw, however, was the widow's peak, revealed when his hat had come off, which completely changed the shape of his face.

She smiled as she looked away from him, relaxing the death grip she'd had on his arm - it might not be so hard to do her duty after all.

Dinner was uneventful, the food excellent. Gwen and Kitty found themselves on either side of the mayor, at the head of the table, surrounded by politicians who were too busy talking amongst themselves to pay much attention to the pilots, besides an occasional polite enquiry. Gwen had been briefed by Kitty, though, so she didn't mind too much; the dinner table wasn't the place for the real conversations - the bargaining, debating and sometimes blackmailing, would take place afterwards, on and around the dance floor.

When dessert was done, Edgerton and Barton reappeared from their places near the foot of the table to claim them and they made their way with everyone else to the ballroom.

Gwen gave Edgerton two dances instead of just one, as much to postpone the ones she was obliged to have with the politicians and businessmen as out of any sense of owing it to him. It went down well with the photographers who had reappeared after the dinner, though, and, when she caught sight of their reflections in the mirrors that lined one side of the large room, she had to admit they made a dashing couple in their uniforms.

It was the mayor's turn next, but, just as he was leading Gwen through the first steps of a foxtrot, the band abruptly stopped playing. However, almost before the echoes of the last trumpet note had faded, they struck up again with a different tune, one that made the mayor let go of her and then turn, along with every other man and woman present, to face the glass doors leading to the garden, or rather the man standing in the opening.

It took very little time for Gwen to recognise the American national anthem and she had no need to wait for the man with the receding hairline and round wire-framed spectacles to be announced to work out that he was Robert Alfred Taft, the President of the United Federation of American States.

Gwen imitated the other military members in the room and respectfully stood rigidly to attention, even though such strict devotion to the anthem had never really been expected in Britain - Queen Victoria, who had commissioned the work from Elgar, had famously said that "The anthem is not mine, or the country's, it belongs to the people and they may treat or mistreat it as they please."

She felt rather than saw someone move up beside her, taking advantage of everyone else being occupied to approach her discreetly, and she spoke to him out of the corner of her mouth without otherwise moving.

'You got in, then.'

'Of course.'

'I haven't seen you.'

'I've been around. Listening. Learning.'

'Eating?'

Gascoyne-Beresford huffed softly. 'I may have picked a few choice morsels from the plates when nobody was looking.'

'What do you make of this, then? I didn't think the President was coming.'

'He wasn't supposed to. He's supposed to be in Caracas for a cabinet meeting tomorrow.'

The anthem reached its climax, a resounding martial crescendo of horns and drums, then ended. The silence after was filled with applause and Gwen relaxed from her at attention position and joined in, but a chill passed through her when the president's eyes fixed firmly on hers and she caught a flash of something in his expression that certainly wasn't in keeping with the festivities. It was only when the clapping finished that he finally looked away and swept his audience with his gaze.

'Thank you, thank you! Please pardon the interruption, but I was in the neighbourhood and felt I had to stop by to say hello. Don't worry I'm not going to make any long speeches about my latest policies, or tell you anything you already know, like why you're here, or how important our guest is.'

Taft paused as soft laughter rang out around the room, but Gwen didn't join in this time.

Neither did Gascoyne-Beresford. 'Did you hear it?' he asked quietly.

'Yes.'

There had been an almost imperceptible pause before Taft had said the word "important", which had only made Gwen feel even colder. A feeling that only intensified when Taft locked eyes with her again.

'I will, however, claim the privilege of a dance before I go on my way.'

The president finally entered the ballroom and walked directly towards Gwen, ignoring the men vying for his attention and the flashes of the cameras, which had abandoned her and the mayor as soon as he had appeared.

'Looks like you're going to get a rare opportunity.' Gascoyne-Beresford said in her ear. 'Don't waste it.' The aide melted away into the crowd, disappearing as unobtrusively as he had appeared, leaving her alone to face Taft's advance.

'Miss Stone, may I?'

Without waiting for an answer or acknowledging the mayor, Taft took Gwen's hand and led her to the very centre of the dance floor. The same foxtrot started up again and he immediately pulled her in and started moving.

His technique was rudimentary and functional and it was immediately obvious that he wasn't dancing with her for the pleasure of it, or for the cameras, which were capturing every moment, but for the chance to speak to her in relative privacy.

'How are you finding our fair country, Miss Stone?'

The seemingly casual question had Gwen's mind racing. In the few days before being packed into the Beagle, she and Kitty had been given a briefing on the places they were going and the people they were likely to meet. They had been inundated with information and she had forgotten most of it, so she didn't recall much of what she'd been told about Taft. The one thing she did remember was that he was supposed to hate small talk, which meant that there had to be something behind his enquiry, after all, the man knew that they had arrived that morning. She couldn't quite work out what, though, so she decided it was best to just answer honestly.

'I haven't had much time to appreciate it yet, but what I've seen so far is certainly impressive.'

'You were here before, weren't you? Didn't your parents show you the sights?'

Again, Gwen hesitated, unsure what he was getting at. 'They did, yes... But I was too young to remember much and we didn't really leave New York anyway. I'm looking forward to seeing what's beyond the city.'

'Oh, America is a large and diverse place, I'm sure you *would* like it.'

Something about the way the man worded his answer struck her as odd and she frowned.

He smirked at her expression. 'Yes, I'm sure you'd like it, *if* you saw any of it. However, I don't think there's much point in you going on with your little tour. You see, I don't intend to let you drag this country onto the losing side of a war.'

He stopped dancing suddenly, dragging her to an abrupt halt. The smirk disappeared, replaced by a wide smile as he turned to face the cameras and pulled her in close by his side.

The flashes of a dozen or so bulbs blinded Gwen and she blinked rapidly. When her eyes finally cleared, she started when Taft spun to face her, thrusting his face in close to hers, and hissed at her.

'We told you to go harder on the Prussians after the first one of these. We told you to break them and make sure they would never come back. You British wouldn't have it, though, so here we are again. And now you expect us to bail you out of another shooting match? One of your own making? I don't think so! It would be best for everyone if you stopped lying to my people, got back in your underwater ship, or whatever you damn Brits call it, and go home. Your mission was a failure before you even got here and you are not welcome.'

He pulled back just far enough to give her a venomous smile, then, with a last wave to the movie cameras and a curt nod to the mayor, he walked away, pausing only to shake hands with Senator Gould before he walked out into the garden, followed by the majority of the photographers and journalists.

Forgotten by everyone, Gwen tottered over to the side of the room and collapsed into one of the chairs around the small tables. She absently took a glass of champagne from a waiter and was just about to down it when Kitty appeared and took it from her hand.

'Now, now. I'm sure that quite a few people will want to talk to you about the great honour you've just been afforded, so you should at least try to keep your wits about you, darling,' the American took a big swig from the flute, then smacked her lips, 'even if this is damn good.'

'Honour? Disaster, more like.'

'What did he say?'

Gwen jumped at the voice, coming from close behind her, and turned to find Gascoyne-Beresford sitting on the chair beside hers at the previously empty table. She looked back to Kitty and scowled. 'Some warning next time?'

Kitty smirked and slipped into the chair next to her. 'Hey, we're on the ground. I don't need to look after your six down here.'

Gwen gave her an evil look, then faced the aide. 'He told me to go home, that the mission was a failure. His words.'

Gascoyne-Beresford chuckled and shook his head. 'Taft trying it on again.'

Kitty raised an eyebrow. 'You seem remarkably unconcerned considering we've just found out the President is firmly against the country helping us.'

Gwen nodded. 'What chance do we have if the President is against us?'

'We already knew that Taft wasn't on our side.' The aide waved his hand dismissively. 'Fortunately, though, as you probably know from the history books, the Americans based their democratic model on the short-lived "United States of America" and the President doesn't have the final say in this kind of thing.'

'Still,' said Kitty, 'there are a lot of politicians who think the same way, who will listen to what he has to say and vote with him.'

'Undoubtedly, but if we are persuasive enough, that number will come down. We also have an "ace in the hole", I believe the term is.' He looked to Kitty for confirmation and she nodded. 'The Senator for Paraguay is on his way back from his tour of Europe. I believe you met him in Gibraltar? Well, he confided to the king that he'll be recommending that America joins the war on our side. Apparently he described both the Kaiser and the Italian Emperor as "power hungry" and was rightly horrified by their cavalier attitude to the suffering they were causing.'

Gascoyne-Beresford looked at Gwen. 'That's still no guarantee, though, so, what you need to do is go dance with as many of these bigwigs as you can, show them the human side of this war. Meanwhile, I'm going to get closer to Senator Gould; I don't know nearly enough about what's making him tick for my liking.'

'What about me?' asked Kitty.

Gascoyne-Beresford paused in the act of getting up from his chair and looked at her in surprise. 'You? Well, I suppose you *could* keep your ear to the ground, but your main job tonight is essentially not to show us up and get your face in the papers tomorrow. Have some fun, if you can, just not too much - I know how you pilots are.' He gave her a warning look, then slipped out of his chair, grabbed the hand of one of the women standing at the side of the room, waiting for partners, gave her one of his most charming smiles, and whirled her out onto the dance floor towards where the senator for New York was dancing with the mayor's wife.

CHAPTER 4

Gwen woke up just after ten the next morning, well-rested, in sharp contrast to Kitty. The American had drunk far too much champagne in between dances, then gotten talked into a poker game in a back room and while she was there she had partaken of even more Kentucky Bourbon, her favourite drink. She had come back to the hotel with a case of the bourbon that the mayor had given her after she'd told him she couldn't get it in Britain anymore and her pockets stuffed with dollar bills, which had previously belonged to a couple of businessmen, a congressman and a senator. Consequently, she was more than a little hungover and wasn't able face the late breakfast they had delivered to their room. Gwen ate heartily, though, wolfing down the bacon sandwiches she'd ordered - her, and most of the RAC's, preferred breakfast before flying - while Kitty retired rapidly to the bathroom, groaning and clutching her stomach.

It had been agreed by both the Americans and British consul that Gwen would turn up for the demonstration flight off the American navy's new aircraft carrier already in her flightsuit. This would give the public their first sight of her in her "work clothes" and the press something different to photograph her in.

It had been almost two months since she'd last flown, on the day they'd fled Gibraltar, and she was itching to get back into an aircraft, even if it wasn't Excalibur. Rarely in her life had she been out of the sky for so long, in fact the only time she'd spent more than a month on the ground since she'd turned six had been when she'd broken her arm falling off a gantry in her workshop at thirteen. Just the act of putting on her flightsuit was bringing it home to her how close she was to doing so and she could feel her heart starting to pump harder in anticipation. Unfortunately, it was also rubbing Kitty's nose into the fact that she wasn't, so she reined in her enthusiasm as much as she could, but there was no way she could hide it entirely and Kitty's mood went from bad to worse.

Gascoyne-Beresford was waiting for them outside the hotel with the consulate's autocar and they piled in for the short ride to the docks.

Even before they had settled in their seats, the aide thrust a small pile of newspapers at them. 'Here you have a good representation of the division present in American society.' He leaned forward and tapped the paper on top. 'Front page headline - "British heroes arrive in New York".' He pulled it away revealing the next. 'Again, front page - "Flyers for Freedom"' He quickly flipped through a couple more. 'As you can see, quite a few of the morning papers have quite rightly put your arrival where it belongs.' He tapped the last of the newspapers. 'That's a lovely picture of the two of you, by the way. Feel free to keep it for your scrapbook.'

He placed those papers aside and took a smaller pile from the seat next to him. 'Then there's these three.' The headline on the first read "Japan Trade Deal Falls Through" and there was no sign of anything about the pilots on the front page. 'The story is in there, but it's been buried and only covered very factually. This one gives it only one paragraph and doesn't mention either of you by name, while the others run the story on pages fifteen and twenty two and dedicate less than half a column.'

He took away those newspapers and placed them on the seat by him, next to the first set. 'Finally we have these.'

He handed them the last pile, which was thicker than the other two. 'These are fervently against America joining the war on our side. Each of them has run the story on the front page above the fold, but the tone of the articles is vastly different from the first ones I showed you. Most of them are against joining the war at all and don't hesitate to express that opinion, however, disturbingly, there are three that advocate allying with the Prussians. Those three have published very similar, very scathing articles with very little in the way of actual reporting, but plenty of diatribe and vitriol, designed, I can only imagine, to stir up some already heated tempers among the middle and lower classes.'

He laid the last lot of newspapers on the seat beside him, creating three neat piles.

'Now, unfortunately, we aren't ever going to change the minds of those who are against us; they're too set in their ways. Neither is there much point in dedicating too much of our time to those who are already on our side, besides what is needed to keep them there.' He laid his hand on the pile in the middle. 'Rather, it's the people sitting on the fence who will be your objectives over the next couple of weeks. Those people don't realise that, as soon as the Prussians are done with us, it will be their turn next. You've made a good start, but it's going to take more than a few smiles and waves to convince them. This morning's flight, for example, is a chance to show them that, while we might be fighting a losing battle at the moment, all is not lost. You need to show them that Britain has warriors that can face up to the Prussians and our request for help doesn't mean that the Americans will be doing all the work themselves, that we don't just want their men to die instead of ours.'

Gwen smiled slowly. 'I think I can do that.'

'Good.' The aide nodded, then looked at Kitty. 'And while Squadron Leader Stone is taking care of things in the air, Lieutenant Wright will be with the press covering the story on the carrier, to answer any questions they might have and enlighten them to how difficult whatever,' he waved his hand vaguely, '*shenanigans* you're carrying out in the air actually are and how few pilots can pull them off.'

Kitty groaned. 'Hoo-bloody-ray. Sounds like fun ...'

Gascoyne-Beresford grinned at her. 'I'm glad you feel that way, because we had a request for an interview from a radio station that happens to be in one of the buildings overlooking the carrier. After the flight, Squadron Leader Stone has a debriefing with the captain of the ship and the admiral of the fleet, with the press attending, of course, which will give you plenty of time to pop over the road.'

Kitty glared at the man, then turned to Gwen. 'Is it too late to resign my commission?'

Gwen chuckled, not unsympathetically. 'I think so, sorry.'

The American thought for a second. 'We could steal a couple of aircraft of the carrier, fly them out into the countryside and lose ourselves in the wilderness for a few weeks.'

Gwen sighed. 'That does sound rather good, but a lot of people are counting on us.'

'For King and Country, eh?' Kitty shook her head. 'Well, next time "Georgey" springs one of these missions on us, remind me to tell him where to stuff it. I'm a pilot, not a,' she waved her hand vaguely at

Gascoyne-Beresford, imitating one of his most annoying mannerisms, 'diplomat.'

'Just as well,' the aide said, 'because right now we need pilots more than we need diplomats. Even ones of my calibre.'

Kitty scoffed, expecting sarcasm, but Gascoyne-Beresford nodded earnestly.

'It's true. A diplomat is useless if he has nothing to back up his words and right now Britain's pilots are the biggest and best bargaining chip we could ever hope for.'

The autocar came to a stop and the man peered out through the darkened windows. 'Ah, here we are. It looks like everything's ready for you. Remember - military discipline today, so loosen up those saluting arms.' He chuckled at his own wit, then sat back, melting into the shadows as the driver opened the door on bright sunlight.

Kitty stepped out and Gwen was about to follow her when Gascoyne-Beresford called out to her.

'Oh, and Squadron Leader?'

'Yes?'

'Try not to make a scene, would you? And don't say anything.'

Gwen frowned, but, before she could asked him what he meant, the first unmistakable notes of the British national anthem sounded and she was forced to scurry to her place next to Kitty.

She stood at attention while the music played, but let her eyes roam around, taking in the spectacle laid out before her.

The Americans had begun a huge military expansion program in response to most of the rest of the world being at war. They had accelerated research, development and building of new weapons, aircraft and vehicles, trying to keep up with the British and Prussians, who were throwing everything they had into trying to outclass each other. At the same time they had also constructed new military facilities across the country to hold those things and train their people to use them. The extensive dockyards around the mouth of the Hudson River were only a very small part of that, as was the ship that was moored in the southernmost dock, the UFS Machu Pichu, the aircraft carrier that was the flagship of the American Atlantic Fleet. The British visit was a perfect opportunity to present both the recently launched ship and the brand new aircraft it carried, not only to the people whose tax money had paid for it, but the rest of the world as well.

The ship formed a solid wall of dull grey metal to her left, rising at least fifty feet above her and stretching off for hundreds of yards in each direction, completely blocking her view of the river, but to her right and front there was a riot of colour. She hadn't been expecting many people to turn up for the event; in her schedule it was listed as just being for the press, also, she hadn't expected a short test flight as having much of a draw for the public. Obviously the Americans had done and they had made provision for it, setting up five long grandstands along the riverfront, facing the ship. They were filled to the brim with people, many of them wearing the flamboyant clothing she'd seen in and around the hotel and quite a few, especially the children, waving flags.

'They've come to see us.' Kitty muttered from the corner of her mouth, her thoughts evidently following the same line as Gwen's. 'Look how many women are in the crowd. They want to see a woman fly a man's weapon.'

'Seems like Gascoyne-Beresford was right to organise those bloody brunches with women's societies. Looks like I'm going to have to go to them after all.'

'And you're going to have to be nice too.'

'I'm always nice.' Gwen growled, but Elgar's stirring music was coming to its final crescendo so she couldn't say any more and instead brought her eyes back to the front, to where a line of dignitaries had formed while the anthem had played. It was a purely military turnout this time, with the port admiral, who'd met the undersea boat the day before, flanked by a second admiral and three captains. It was an impressive amount of gold braid to meet a pair of pilots, even a pair of Misfits, but, she supposed, the Americans were playing up as much to their audience as to the British, and there were just as many cameras clicking and whirring as there had been at the mayor's reception. At least, she thought, there was a distinct lack of politicians, which would hopefully mean more direct speaking and less interminable speeches.

The final notes of the anthem were greeted by polite applause from the audience, but it lasted only a few seconds before the military band in American naval whites broke out into something a bit more crowd-pleasing. This appeared to be the cue for the five naval officers and they took four steps forwards in unison and came to a smart halt within easy conversational range.

Gwen saluted, seeing Kitty follow suit out of the corner of her eye, and the gesture was reciprocated by the Americans before the admiral they hadn't met before offered her his hand. 'Jefferson Peters, commanding the Atlantic Fleet. Pleased to make your acquaintance, ma'am.'

'Squadron Leader Stone, sir.' She smiled. 'But I think I can assume you already knew that.'

He smiled back at her. 'That's right, ma'am.' He indicated his companions. 'Admiral Jackson you already know.'

'Sir.' Gwen nodded to the port admiral.

'And these are Fleet Captain Silva, Captain Fernández, who commands the Machu Pichu, and Captain Strong, the CAG.'

Gwen nodded to each of them in turn as well, including Captain Strong, even though she had no idea what a CAG was.

'And this,' he gestured towards the waterfront, 'is our pride and joy.'

At this invitation, Gwen turned to get her first proper look at the aircraft carrier. It was huge, far bigger than the HMS Heart of Oak, the largest carrier that Britain had in its arsenal. The ship itself didn't interest her very much, though, it was what she carried that did and she craned her head to gaze up towards the flight deck, but it was too high.

Admiral Peters chuckled. 'I can see you're as eager to get your hands on the Corsario as I am to hear your opinion of what our top designers have come up with, so, shall we head up?'

A gangplank festooned with flags took them, and the gaggle of journalists trailing them, to a hatch in the side of the ship and into the bowels of the vessel.

The interior was much the same as any other military ship that Gwen had ever been on, with metal walls, floors and ceilings, but there was an all-pervading odour that was becoming increasingly familiar to her the more time she spent in America.

'Why does the ship smell so strongly of gasoline?' she asked Kitty. 'Do they use it to cook? Are we near the kitchens?'

Admiral Peters heard her and answered, grinning over his shoulder at them as he led them through the ship. 'We don't use gasoline for cooking, no. That would be unsavoury. We run a cable to the power grid while we're in port, but this girl is powered by some of the most advanced and powerful gasoline engines known to man. That's what you can smell.'

'How can you stand it? I can hardly breathe.'

The admiral shrugged and kept walking. 'You get used to it. After a while you don't notice it.'

After climbing what must have been a dozen flights of stairs, making the journalists huff and puff and Gwen feel decidedly warm in her flightsuit, the party emerged into bright sunshine through a hatch in the side of the "island", the large tower that rose above the Machu Pichu's flight deck.

The view of the city and out over the bay to the south was spectacular, but Gwen didn't see it, instead, her eyes immediately shot to the two aircraft in the dark blue livery of the American navy, sitting a short way to the left of them in the middle of the runway.

She stumbled to a halt and gaped at them.

'What...? That's... They're...' she snarled. 'Damn that man. So that's what he meant.'

She felt Kitty come up beside her. 'Gwen. They look like...'

'Excalibur.' Gwen forced the name of her beloved aircraft out from between her clenched teeth. 'Yes. And Gascoyne-Beresford knew. He told me not to make a scene.'

The aide had caught up with the group half way up the stairs and she searched him out among them and glared at him, but he shook his head and put a finger to his lips. That just served to infuriate her more, but, luckily, Captain Strong was addressing the press, talking about the new fighters they were there to see, and nobody noticed her lapse in composure.

'I'm going to get a closer look.'

'I'll come with you.'

Gwen barely registered Kitty's words as she stomped towards the Corsarios; her full attention was reserved for them.

The aircraft were almost identical to that of her own. The wings were bent in exactly the same place and at exactly the same angle, the tail was just as long and the vertical stabiliser just as high. The armament looked like it was different, though, with fewer gun ports in the wings, and the airscrew wasn't quite as large as Excalibur's either, but those were minor details and did nothing to detract from the fact that the Americans had quite obviously copied, no, *stolen*, her design. Stolen her aircraft.

'Beautiful, aren't they?'

Gwen spun at the sound of the familiar voice and found Lieutenant Barton, the man who had escorted Kitty to the mayor's reception. Like her, he was dressed in a flightsuit.

'They certainly are,' she replied slowly, pointedly, drawing an amused snort from Kitty.

Barton didn't notice anything untoward about her reply, though, and continued to gaze lovingly at the aircraft. 'They're so different from anything else we've ever had and so much better.'

'Really?' Gwen drawled, still seething. 'I'm glad you like them.'

'All the pilots on the Machu Pichu do.' Barton said, nodding enthusiastically, oblivious to the not especially well hidden meaning behind her words.

Kitty stared at him. 'You really don't know, do you?' She looked at Gwen. 'He really doesn't know.'

Barton frowned. 'Know what?'

Kitty raised her eyebrows, wordlessly asking Gwen what she wanted to do, but Gwen just shrugged and turned back to Barton. 'Never mind.' She changed the subject, putting the design theft out of her mind as best she could, at least for the moment. 'So, I take it you'll be coming up with me.'

'The plan is for you to fly around for ten minutes or so, do some aerobatics if you like, then for me to join you for some dogfighting. Sorry.'

'Why "sorry"?'

'Well, because ten minutes isn't nearly enough time to figure out what she's capable of, while I have more than a hundred hours on her. It won't exactly be a fair fight.'

It wasn't the young man's fault, but, given the context that apparently only she and Kitty were aware of, Gwen was finding everything he was saying rather amusing and could barely keep herself from laughing. 'Don't worry on my account. I'll be fine. And please,' she said with a sideways look at Kitty, who was apparently having an even harder time controlling herself, 'don't go easy on me.'

'Ok, then!' Barton grinned, but then stepped back and stiffened to attention. 'Sir!'

'As you were, Lieutenant.' Captain Strong had finished his presentation to the increasingly bored-looking press and had brought everyone over to join the pilots. 'Everything ready?'

'Yes, sir.'

The Captain turned to Gwen. 'Squadron Leader, would you care to evaluate one of our airplanes?'

He presented the question formally, almost stiffly, obviously playing up for the cameras since everybody already knew exactly why she was there. However, Gwen wasn't sure if the mischievous glint in his eye was purely because of that, or whether he was also aware that she had no need to get anywhere near the aircraft to know how it would perform.

She raised her eyebrow slightly and gave him a half smile as she replied, equally formally. 'I'd be delighted, sir.'

'Thank you. Lieutenant Barton will show you your aircraft.'

The man's turn of phrase and the slight emphasis he put on the words "your aircraft" left Gwen with no doubt this time - he knew that the Corsario had been copied from Excalibur. She still said nothing, though, as Gascoyne-Beresford had requested of her, but that didn't mean she wouldn't have some choice words for him afterwards.

'Thank you, sir.' She gave him her best basic training salute, not the casual one she usually threw, holding it slightly longer than necessary, both to drive in that she understood the artifice of the situation and so that the cameras could capture the moment, then did a smart about turn and walked off towards the aircraft. The effect was spoiled somewhat by the fact that she was less walking than waddling because of the liquid pockets in the legs of her flightsuit, but she consoled herself by thinking that it could have been worse - the long leather coat thankfully covered her rear and prevented her from making more of a spectacle of herself than she would have liked to. She did, however, remove the coat as soon as she was at the aircraft, *airplanes*, as the Americans called them, handing it off to one of the fitters, so that the press could get their pictures of her in her "business clothes" with the aircraft.

Barton accompanied her on an inspection of the exterior of the aircraft, walking next to her while she checked it over.

As she manipulated the control surfaces, she could hear Captain Strong explaining what she was doing to the journalists. She grinned when one of them asked if she didn't trust the mechanics, but then realised something, which caused her to frown and take a step back from the machine.

'Is something wrong?' Barton peered at the spot on the wing where she'd been.

'Sorry, what?' She gave him a reassuring smile. 'Oh, no, it's nothing. I'm just... uh... taking my time to appreciate the aircraft.'

She went back to her inspection, but as she continued she did so with as much of an eye for the design as for whether everything was working as it was supposed to.

'So,' she glanced at Barton as she moved round to the back of the aircraft to check the rudder, 'what does "CAG" mean?'

'Commander, Air Group. It's the abbreviation of Captain Strong's title and what we call the officer in that position.'

'Ah. Good.'

'Good?'

'Well,' she leaned in to whisper, 'I thought it was something rude in Spanish.'

Barton snorted. 'No, but, believe me, we call him worse behind his back sometimes.'

'I think that's all servicemen and women have in common.' Gwen said, thinking not about Abby, but about the War Minister. The Misfits frequently had bad things to say about him and never jokingly, which was often the case when soldiers complained about their superiors.

She finished the walk around, but before she climbed up into the cockpit to do the last checks she turned to Barton.

'Anything I need to know about how she handles? Does she maybe have a few problems at low speed?'

While the overall design of the Corsario was the same as Excalibur's, many of the small details differed to varying degrees, for instance, the tail was a few inches shorter and the control surfaces were slightly different sizes. The majority of these changes were distinctly sub-optimal and Gwen was puzzled as to why they had been implemented because they would reduce the aircraft's overall performance. None of them was particularly serious and as a whole they wouldn't result in the aircraft being bad, but there was one thing that she was extremely worried about and it wasn't so much a change as an omission. Back when she'd first flown Excalibur she'd had some distinctly life-threatening handling problems. Those had been solved with a small stall bar on the right wing, but that bar was conspicuously absent on the Corsario.

Barton blinked at her. 'How did you...?' He shook his head and grinned wryly. 'I was told you were a designer and I should have expected as much, I suppose.' He reached out to pat the side of the aircraft. 'Yes, you're right, of course, she does have a few... foibles, shall we say? She can be a bit temperamental at low speeds and she doesn't like being put in a spin.'

'Alright, don't put her into a spin and, what?' she grinned. 'Don't land?'

Barton laughed. 'It's not hard to predict when she's going to misbehave when you get used to her, but we've arranged for you to land at the air division's airstrip across the river. It's long enough to land their big cargo planes, so you won't have to get anywhere near a stall.'

Gwen thought back to how Excalibur had handled before she'd solved the low-speed handling problems. It would be much safer not to land on the carrier, but that might give the impression to the press and audience that she was somehow inferior to the American pilots. She shook her head. 'That's not necessary. I'll land here.'

'You have to be carrier certified for that, ma'am, I'm sorry...'

'I *am* carrier certified. I've made several hundred landings on the Arturo and she has a wire capture system identical to yours.'

She didn't tell him that the vast majority of those landings had been on a mock-up of the Arturo drawn out on the landing field of the Bagshot Estate and that she'd only actually landed on the Arturo a handful of times. She figured that it didn't actually matter; hitting the wire on the Machu Pichu, which was currently sitting perfectly still and not bobbing up and down or steaming at full speed would be more like landing on the grass than the Arturo.

'I'll have to check with the CAG, ma'am.'

'Please do.'

As Barton hurried away towards the officers, Gwen clambered up onto the wing and peered into the cockpit. As she'd suspected, the layout was completely different to hers. There was even a stick instead of the yoke she used.

The aircraft shifted, letting her know that someone was coming up onto the wing with her, but it wasn't Barton coming back, it was Kitty.

'Are you going to be able to fly this thing?'

'You've seen it too, then?'

The American nodded. 'What did they do, do you think? Copy a photograph from a newspaper?'

Gwen shook her head. 'No, they bought one of John Dunne's models from Hamleys. He told me that the demand for Excalibur models was so high he'd had to use some parts from a batch of mark one Harridans just to keep up. They're not a perfect match, but close enough to use with only a bit of alteration.' She jerked her chin at the right wing. 'The model doesn't have the stall strip either.'

Kitty looked down at the wing. 'Oh, for... and they let them land these things on carriers?'

'Apparently so.'

Kitty gestured towards the group standing by the tower. Captain Strong had finished his presentation a while ago and was in conference with Barton while the fleet captain, Captain Peters, addressed the journalists, who were paying him about as much attention as they had Strong, which was to say not much. 'From what they said, I get the impression that they've rather rushed these aircraft into service.'

'Bloody irresponsible.' Gwen growled.

'I take it they're not expecting you to land here.'

Gwen leaned into the cockpit to study the instruments, so that she didn't need to meet Kitty's eyes as she answered. 'No, they've arranged for me to use an airstrip belonging to their air division across the river.'

'Good. Well, at some point the brass are going to stop boring the press to death and they'll undoubtedly want to bombard me with questions, so I should be getting back. Take care up there.'

Gwen straightened up and smiled at her. 'I will.'

They surreptitiously held hands for a few seconds before Kitty jumped down from the wing and sauntered back to the group, passing the returning Barton on the way. The navy pilot looked up at her over the front of the wing.

'The CAG says you can land here if you've got that much carrier experience, but, and I quote, "on your head be it".'

'Thank you.'

Barton nodded. 'Good luck and see you in the air, ma'am.' He smiled, then went to his own aircraft to begin his checks.

A fitter climbed up next to her and helped her to get settled in her seat. While he was tightening her straps and connecting her to the radio and heating, she scanned the instruments and moved her hands around the controls to familiarise herself with them.

The layout might have been different to hers, but all cockpits followed a certain logic and it didn't take long for her to get used to it. Final checks took only a minute more, then the fitter tapped the side of her cockpit to show he was as happy as she was before jumping down.

'Machu Pichu control, this is Badger Two, ready for takeoff.'

The radio station that would interview Kitty was providing a commentary on her flight, which included broadcasting her communications, so it had been decided that it would be a good idea for Gwen to use the Misfit callsign she was widely known by. That was fine by her; not only was she comfortable with it, but you never knew what embarrassing name someone else would come up with.

'Roger, Badger Two. Stand by, please.'

'Badger Two standing by.'

The controller sounded exasperated and a quick glance through the windshield showed Gwen why. While the journalists were still with the officers by the island, the photographers had spread out across the flight deck as they vied for clear sightlines or an interesting angle. They were now being rounded up by a group of grinning sailors and herded like sheep back to the side of the deck, from where they would have a clear view without being in danger. It took quite a while for them to get out of the way because some of the movie cameras were quite heavy and decidedly unwieldy, but finally the wonderfully clear speakers in her new helmet came to life again.

'Badger Two, this is Machu Pichu control. You are cleared for takeoff. Wind is at five knots from the south east. Have a good flight.'

'Thank you, Machu Pichu control.'

Gwen met the eye of the man standing ready in front of her aircraft and he nodded, then called out to his team. The Corsario shifted as his team pushed it into the middle of the deck and turned it to face down the runway.

The signals the man gave her to apply her brakes, release the spring and throttle up were unfamiliar, but perfectly understandable, especially given that she knew what she had to do already. However, the flamboyant shooting motion he made when it was time for her to go made her laugh, so much so that it took her a couple of seconds of fumbling to release the brakes, forcing him to hold his ridiculous position longer than he should have. He was wobbling unsteadily in a long lunge position as she powered past him and she shot him an apologetic grin before leaving him behind.

The runway on the Machu Pichu was much longer than the Arturo and, even though she'd started from just under half way, she still had almost as much room for the aircraft to get to takeoff speed. That was just as well, though, because it took her all of a heartbeat to realise that the Corsario was rather underpowered due to a smaller, basic airscrew and an American spring, which were typically much weaker than British and Prussian ones. The aircraft needed nearly fifty feet more than Excalibur did to reach a safe takeoff speed and she gave it a few dozen more, just to be safe, before pulling back smoothly on the stick.

She ran through a basic series of manoeuvres to get the hang of the aircraft in the guise of a couple of flybys for the audience, but then she took it up to a couple of thousand feet over the bay and threw the throttle wide to really see what it could do and give the crowd something to watch.

Despite that lack of power and a noticeable loss of responsiveness due to the mismatched control surfaces, the Corsario was still close enough to Excalibur's design for it to be an excellent aircraft and it was a joy to fly. She found herself getting lost in the flight as she developed an understanding with the machine and it was a shock to her when her headphones crackled, meaning she'd been in the air ten minutes already.

'Badger Two, this is Inca One. Are you ready to have some fun?'

Gwen glanced down at the carrier just in time to see the other Corsario taking to the sky and grinned. She didn't think telling him that the dogfight wasn't going to be much fun, at least for him, would be a good idea over the open channel with who knew how many people listening, so she just replied normally. 'Roger, Inca. Ready when you are.'

She put the aircraft into a lazy turn, holding position and conserving spring tension while Barton climbed to meet her.

'Ok,' Barton said as he pulled up on her left wing, 'rules are we stay above one thousand feet and over the bay. Either of us strays below that or over the land we stop and reset. Got it?'

'Understood, Inca.'

'Head on, passing to the right?'

'Sounds good to me.'

'Ok. Break and turn back on my mark.'

'Roger.'

There was an etiquette to practice dogfights. Unless you were setting up a specific scenario, like being bounced by an enemy coming from the sun, the standard start was for the two aircraft to go head to head, which made the fight even off the bat.

Gwen made a sharp ninety-degree turn to the right as Barton did the same to the left and they flew directly away from each other. She watched the American's aircraft receding in the mirror above her head. It was almost too small to see before Barton gave the order.

'Mark!'

Gwen banked the aircraft to point back the way she'd come and threw the throttle wide open.

'Alright then, Lieutenant,' she muttered to herself after she closed the channel, 'let's see if you know your aircraft half as well as you think you do.'

Her "enemy" was nothing more than a dot in the centre of her windscreen, but with the two aircraft racing towards each other at speeds approaching their best it expanded rapidly.

A head on attack was a risky proposition in actual combat circumstances. Far too many pilots had misjudged things and ended up colliding with the bomber they'd been targeting, especially in the desperate days of September of the year before and even the most experienced pilots were hesitant to carry out the manoeuvre as the margin for error was so small as to be all but non-existent. Much of that risk was neutralised in a practice dogfight, though, because the pilots agreed beforehand how they were going to pass each other and

Gwen touched her rudder pedals gently to place Barton's aircraft slightly off to the left of her sights.

It was a matter of seconds to close the distance and the other Corsario flashed past, seemingly close enough to touch, but in reality there had been a good two wingspans between them.

An inexperienced pilot, one who hadn't been in hundreds, if not thousands, of dogfights, who hadn't seen every reaction possible to every possible scenario and hadn't replayed those scenarios in their head over and over, would naturally throw their aircraft into the hardest turn they possibly could in an effort to come around onto the tail of their opponent. If both pilots did that then the fight would come down to whose aircraft could turn the hardest, something that was redundant in a fight involving two identical machines and would only result in a stalemate. Gwen wasn't, in any conceivable manner, an inexperienced pilot and, as soon as she'd seen Barton put his aircraft into a maximum rate turn in the mirror above her head, she inverted the Corsario and pulled the stick back as hard as she could.

She immediately lost sight of Barton, but that didn't bother her; she knew exactly where he'd be if he kept going how she expected he would. It took only a few seconds for her to find him again and she grinned wryly and shook her head when she saw that he was holding his turn.

The G forces were fierce, but she stuck with her inverted loop, adjusting her course to track Barton. Popping up behind him was a simple matter and she stuck with him through his attempts to shake her off, easily staying within optimal cannon range.

'Takatakatakatakatakataka,' she called out with a grin, thinking back to all the times she'd heard the same thing from Abby. However, while her friend took practice dogfights very seriously and didn't hold back on letting her victims know very clearly that they were "dead", Gwen would not and could not crow over her defeated foe, instead she had to tread a fine line. She wanted the listeners to know that she was the superior pilot, but didn't want them to think she was being boastful, or taking a malicious delight in an American's inferiority. She also didn't want Barton to become resentful, which was why she'd tried to make the noise as playfully as she could.

It didn't take long for the American to give up his evasive efforts and she pulled up beside him again. Thankfully, his grin as he looked over at her seemed genuine, without any rancour at being beaten.

'Ok, Badger, it was close, but I'll give you that one.'

Gwen laughed as he winked at her. 'Very generous of you, Inca.'

'Shall we go again?'

'With pleasure.'

Without waiting for the order, Gwen stood the aircraft on its wing and pulled a sharp ninety degree turn.

Barton had very obviously underestimated her during the first dogfight, but he didn't make the same mistake again. However, no matter how hard he tried Gwen easily managed to defeat him every time, not that he was bad, by any means, he was actually very good and she could see why they had chosen him to represent them, but he lacked her experience and familiarity with the aircraft. After four combats she was running too low on tension to safely do another. However, instead of being disappointed that her fun was ending, she was glad, because, even though she had been told to show how good she was, she wouldn't have liked to humiliate the young man or destroy his confidence in his abilities.

Despite the misgivings of the Americans, putting down on the deck of the Machu Pichu was a simple proposition for her and she snagged the third wire with ease.

The press swarmed around the aircraft as soon as the ground crew had declared it safe for them to do so and the fitter who was helping her detach herself from the aircraft chuckled. 'Bit more interested now, aren't they, ma'am? Now everyone's seen what you can do and they've got a story.' He finished his work and tapped the side of the cockpit. 'Damn good flying, ma'am.' He gave her a nod, then jumped down from the wing and hurried off, leaving her to the cameras.

The Misfits were used to getting attention from the press in England. Whenever they made a public appearance they were always among the most photographed people, almost on a par with the Royal Family. The American press were something else, though. They weren't particularly civilised for a start, shouting out requests for her to turn and pose and smile and wave without any semblance of order, sometimes shouting over each other in their attempts to make themselves heard. She did her best to accommodate them but some of the things they wanted her to do were improper to say the least and some were downright indecent. They certainly weren't appropriate for an officer in the RAC. There were very few questions from the journalists, which she found surprising, and those were all along the lines of "you gotta boyfriend, darling?" or worse, which told her both that their articles were going to be more akin to the ones run in the tabloids back home than anything to do with the mission or the aircraft and that they hadn't bothered to read the press releases that the British

Consulate had given out, which had background information on her and Kitty.

Eventually the photographers tired, or had what they needed, and began to pack up their cameras. That seemed to be the signal for things to finish and Captain Strong stepped forwards and faced them.

'Ladies and Gentlemen, that concludes...'

'One last question, please, Captain!'

Strong blinked in surprise. 'Really? Oh, OK, please, go ahead.'

Gwen searched out the man who had spoken up and found him a few yards behind the group. That puzzled her slightly - most of the men and women of the press had jostled for position around her, vying for her attention or searching for the best angle for their images, but he evidently didn't care to do so, in fact his hands were in his pockets, rather than clutching a camera or a notebook. His attitude was strange too; he was slouched nonchalantly and there was a sardonic smile curling his lip up to one side.

'You have a question, Mr...?'

'Jones. Aviation Weekly. And yes, I do, Squadron Leader. If you don't mind.'

Many of the journalists showed signs of impatience, rolling their eyes, not very subtly checking their watches, or shifting impatiently, but Gwen smiled at him, fairly sure she knew what was coming. The others would have no clue that the Corsario was a copy of Excalibur, but he certainly would; his magazine had covered much of the air war over Europe and clippings of the articles were prized possessions among many British pilots.

'Of course not, ask away.'

'Thanks. I just wanted to know - what did you think of the Corsario?'

'Well, Mr Jones, the Corsario is very good. Very fast and very agile. In fact, it handles very much like my own aircraft.'

'You don't say.' He drawled, grinning.

Gwen stifled a laugh and gave him a nod, which he returned before looking away to watch the fitters fold the wings of Barton's aircraft and manhandle it towards one of the lifts that connected with the hangar deck.

There was a moment of silence as everyone waited to see if Jones had finished and when neither he nor Gwen said anything else Captain Strong cleared his throat.

'Well. As I was saying, that concludes our demonstration. Refreshments have been laid on in the officer's mess and some of our pilots will be on hand to answer any questions you might have. This way, please.'

The men and women of the press moved off, showing more enthusiasm than they had for the navy's presentation and in short order the flight deck was cleared of all non-military personnel.

Barton wandered over, shaking his head. 'I heard you Misfits were good, but I thought it was just because you flew custom planes. I had no idea...'

There was no modest answer to that, so Gwen just smiled and waited for him to go on.

'I didn't have a chance up there. I couldn't get close to you! And some of the things you made her do... Even I didn't know she could do all that! How... How did you do that? How did you *know* she could do that? My God, if the Prussians are even half as good as you, what chance do American pilots have if we join the war?'

Gwen grimaced; it looked like she had gone much further in destroying the young man's confidence than she'd realised.

Despite Gascoyne-Beresford's warning not to say anything she just couldn't keep quiet. Who knew how much damage could be done if rumours of a supposed superiority of European pilots spread throughout the American armed forces.

She grabbed Barton's arm and pulled him away from the aircraft, out of the hearing of the men working on it. 'Believe me, the Prussians are nowhere near as good as the Misfits, not even Gruber and his squadron, but I didn't beat you because you're a worse pilot than I am, I beat you because I *do* know the Corsario. A lot better than you ever could.'

'How in hell...?'

Gwen cut him off with a shake of the head. 'You'll find out eventually, I reckon, but it's not my place to tell you.' She glanced up as a sailor came out of the bridge tower and started walking purposely towards them. Knowing she wouldn't have much longer alone with Barton she fixed him with her eyes and spoke as earnestly as she could. 'Look, don't read too much into today; it doesn't mean anything.'

That was all she had time to say before the sailor came to a halt beside them and saluted smartly. 'Squadron Leader Stone?'

She returned the gesture, careful not to strike the mechanism of her new American lenses. 'Yes?'

'I was asked to escort you to the ready room by the CAG, ma'am. Lieutenant Wright and your assistant, uh, Mr Gasket, had to go, but they left you this.'

He held up Gwen's small kitbag containing her dress uniform and she stifled a smile as she took it from him, storing away his error for later enjoyment with Kitty. 'Thank you, I'll be with you presently.'

'Ma'am.' The man nodded, then backed away until he was out of earshot and studiously stared at a point on the horizon out over the bay.

She turned back to Barton. 'I have to go, but I just want to say one thing first...' She nodded at the Corsario, 'a stall strip on the wing will solve the low speed handling problems.'

She gave him one last smile, then strode away before he could question her further.

CHAPTER 5

'I had to, don't you see?' Gwen told the frowning Gascoyne-Beresford later, in the autocar on the way back to the hotel. 'Not "making a scene" about having my design stolen is one thing, not giving them a simple solution to a design flaw which could cost lives is completely different.'

The aide stared at her for a long moment, but then his expression suddenly brightened and he flashed her his brilliant smile. 'Not to worry; I'll just make sure that the right ears are whispered in and we'll turn this to our advantage.' He sat up, excited all of a sudden. 'It might even be enough to knock one or two of those people off the fence and into our garden! Well done, Squadron Leader, well done indeed!'

The sailor had taken Gwen from the flight deck to the pilots' ready room, directly below the bridge tower, and had stood guard outside the door of the bathroom while she showered and changed.

Most of the British warships she had been on made some concessions for the comfort of the crew. The Arturo had been the most extreme example, having been a cruise liner before being repurposed, but even the newest additions to the fleet, like the Heart of Oak and the Steady, which had been built with being the most efficient tools of war possible were far more welcoming than the Machu Pichu. The ready room was in keeping with the stark nature of the rest of the ship, with the thinnest of carpets on the metal deck, not a single painting or anything beyond a clock to relieve the grey paint of the metal walls, and no sign of a tea urn. The bathroom itself lacked even the carpet and the floor was icy as she undressed and stepped into the shower. Thankfully, though, the water was piping hot and the pressure decent, so she soon had the small room filled with steam as she cleaned away the sweat created by her exertions in the air.

She had never been one of those girls who took hours to shower and fix her hair and makeup and in less than twenty minutes she was ready to face the final and by far the least enjoyable part of her duties that morning.

She had been dreading making smalltalk with the journalists, fearing letting slip something she shouldn't, or having something she said taken out of context and used against her, or her country, in the papers. In the end she needn't have worried, because when she arrived at the officer's mess she found it empty except for a half-dozen rather shell-shocked looking stewards, who were dealing with what looked like the aftermath of a stampede. Hardly any food was left on the large buffet table set out in the centre of the room and what little there was wasn't in any real condition to eat, having been pawed at or knocked around by grabbing hands. She was beginning to despair of finding something to replace the copious amounts of energy she'd burnt before she felt adverse effects when one of the stewards beckoned to her. He took her to one of several small booths, much like the ones in American "diners" and lifted a big tray from where it had been concealed beneath the thinly-padded bench. He placed it on the table for her and lifted the metal lids from the plates to reveal a wide selection of foods.

'What would you like to drink, ma'am? Can I get you some tea? Orange juice? Perhaps some bitter? We have some imported from England that you might enjoy.'

Gwen found that she was inordinately pleased that the Americans had taken the trouble to find out what she liked to drink, although it was slightly worrying at the same time that such personal information about her was so readily available. It was a bit too early in the day to start consuming alcohol, though, much as she felt like it at that moment. 'Tea would be lovely, thank you, and some water, if it's not too much trouble.'

'Coming right up, ma'am.'

After Gwen had consumed a large proportion of the contents of the tray and pushed it away, the sailor had reappeared and taken her down through the ship to the gangway out onto the dock.

With the display long over, most of the spectators had already gone, but several dozen people had lingered. They were in a loose group in front of the nearest grandstand, prevented from wandering any closer to the carrier by a rope that had been tied between two convenient lampposts and being watched over by four sailors.

The Misfits were always being asked for autographs whenever they appeared in public, but the British were rather more restrained than the Americans, who began shouting as soon as they saw her and pushing against the rope in an attempt to get to her. The sailors were struggling to contain them so she hurried over, hoping to relieve the pressure on them. It didn't work, though, and they continued to jostle each other to get closer to her, even as she frantically signed whatever they thrust at her. It wasn't until she'd done the majority of them that the sailors were able to relax, panting from their exertions and, after she signed the last of the autographs, a photograph held out to her by a tall grey-haired man with square glasses, she thanked them.

That was when Kitty and Gascoyne-Beresford had chosen to return and they had bundled Gwen into the consulate's autocar before the autograph hunters could spot the American and return. The aide had asked her how the flight had gone, probably more to be polite than out of any real interest, and that was when she'd told him about the advice she'd given to Barton in parting. That particular subject had been dealt with in a manner that made both her and Gascoyne-Beresford happy, however the aide's smile disappeared when she leaned forward in her seat to confront him about the other thing weighing on her mind.

'How long have you known about the Corsario? How long has the consul? For that matter, does the king know?'

'We've known since before the first aircraft was launched and of course the king has been informed.'

'And?'

'And *nothing*, Squadron Leader. Or do you think that causing an incident over copying your magnificent steed, something that is, I'm sorry, rather insignificant in the grand scheme of things, is worth jeopardising a possible alliance with one of the most powerful countries in the world?'

Gascoyne-Beresford's tone was light and his expression jovial, but there was a hardness in his eyes that made Gwen reconsider what she'd been about to say and remain silent.

'I can see that you are not entirely satisfied with that,' the aide continued, 'and I fully understand. So I will add this - yes, we did have a word with the Americans about their theft, but they started to get a bit uppity and the War Ministry ordered us not to pursue the matter any further. So, that is that, and I would advise you to let it slide.'

Although it was phrased as a suggestion, it was obvious that the aide was as good as ordering her not to say anything to anyone and she hated to admit it, but she had to agree with him. Much as she'd like to shout out to the world what the Americans had done, it wouldn't do anything to help the mission and accusations of theft might in fact turn the public against them.

The truth would come out at some point, anyway, it couldn't not do, what with photographs of Excalibur already published in several periodicals, including that of Mr Jones. He might even make some mention of it in whatever article he published about the day's events.

There was nothing for it but to accept the situation so she nodded to show her acquiescence.

'Good! Well, despite your little indiscretion, this morning has been as successful as I'd hoped. Lieutenant Wright has charmed the airwaves while Squadron Leader Stone has ruled the air from the waves, so to speak! Ha ha!'

He laughed at his own joke, but didn't seem to notice or care that they didn't join in and just went on as before. 'Unfortunately, while it was certainly worth doing, this morning won't further our cause very much. A similar success at the ball this evening definitely will, though, so you'll have to work hard to charm the socks off everybody.'

He tutted and shook his head when Gwen glared at him.

'Oh, don't look at me that way, Squadron Leader. I'm not asking you to do anything so gauche as to sing your own praises like an American - that will be up to the consul and I. It is expected for us to lay it on thick, but for you to do so would be frowned upon and out of character. Or at least out of the character that we want to sell them of the wholesome and virtuous, self-effacing, yet so very capable, British warrior woman. No, you and Lieutenant Wright just have to continue to be your usual selves.'

He held up one of the newspapers from before, one of a few that had run a photograph of Gwen with the President on their front page.

'Last night was just a warm up for the main act tonight. Last night you were among friends and sympathisers, well, mostly anyway. It was more about giving the press some nice photographs and announcing your arrival than making converts. The President messed that up a bit, but it still served its purpose. Tonight, though, you'll be in a far more hostile environment. Not quite Kent last summer, or even Malta, but definitely akin to a foray over France. You'll have some allies in the room and they'll be briefed to step in if need be, but I'd much prefer it if you fended for yourselves and they didn't have to.'

'Will it be that bad?' asked Gwen.

Gascoyne-Beresford nodded. 'Yes.'

The aide wasn't wrong and at times during the couple of hours or so before dinner Gwen did very much feel like she was in the middle of a dogfight - isolated and outnumbered. Attacks came from all sides it seemed in the form of thinly veiled insults, sneers, or whispers behind hands. One woman even disdainfully asked her, to general amusement, why she wasn't leaving the fighting to the men and keeping her home in order for her husband's return. That was easily replied to, though, taking into consideration what had happened to her husband, and it won her quite a few points as many of her detractors backed off in shame.

Constantly being on her guard was exhausting and, as soon as she had a chance, she retreated to the bar at the side of the room and eyed the champagne longingly while she sipped a root beer.

That evening's party was a fundraiser being held in the Science Museum on Fifth Avenue, directly opposite the airship terminal. The main reception was taking place in the large vestibule, where, coincidentally and appropriately, the powered glider that the Wright brothers had flown was on display, hanging from the girders of the steel and glass domed roof. Adjoining rooms to each side served as a ballroom and a dining room. The "ballroom" had been emptied of its exhibitions for the night, but the "dining room" was a permanent display of an enormous Faraday cage, fully twenty yards wide by ten high. The cage took up most of the large room and was designed to hold hundreds of people at a time so the dining table easily fit inside. She just hoped they would turn the exhibition off during the meal because the electricity arcing and cracking overhead would make conversation somewhat difficult and probably not do those men and women with nervous dispositions much good.

The guests had been given free roam of the museum for the night and Gwen and Kitty had wanted to take advantage of that, but Gascoyne-Beresford had shot down that idea, insisting that Gwen remain available for whoever wanted to speak to her, no matter their intentions. Which was why she had escaped to the bar rather than running off to the aviation display on the fourth floor as soon as she had the chance.

'You don't seem to be having much fun, Squadron Leader.'

Gwen turned at the sound of the American accented voice and found a tall man casually leaning against the bar beside her. He was in his fifties, wearing glasses and with grey hair swept back from a widow's peak. He seemed vaguely familiar and she smiled at him, assuming he was one of the allies Gascoyne-Beresford had mentioned, coming to give her a respite.

'Not really, but these kind of things aren't exactly my cup of tea at the best of times, Mr...?'

'Stern. Fred Stern, at your service. And yes, I must say you did look far more comfortable in the air this morning. Impressive display, well done.'

'Thank you. Oh!' The words combined with the distinctive square glasses Stern was wearing gave Gwen the clues she needed to realised where she had seen him before - his had been the last autograph she had signed that morning.

He smiled. 'I see you remember me. We didn't have much of a chance to speak this morning, but perhaps you would honor me with a dance so that we can get better acquainted?'

'I'd be delighted.'

He offered his arm and Gwen took hold of his elbow and let him lead her into the ballroom.

The orchestra had been set up on a balcony, leaving the entire space open for the dancers, but there were only three other couples there at that moment, which left plenty of room for Stern to immediately whirl her into the Viennese waltz that was already in progress. She thanked the fact that she'd had a good few hours to wear in her new boots and get used to them, otherwise the sudden movement might well have resulted in some extremely inelegant and embarrassing stumbling, giving her detractors more ammunition to fire at her.

They danced for a while, getting used to the rhythm and becoming accustomed to each other as partners, before Stern spoke. 'You seem to be making good progress with your mission, Squadron Leader.'

'It's still early days, and please, call me Gwen.'

Stern smiled and nodded. 'The one big obstacle I see, Gwen, is the President being so firmly against you. Have you been told why that is?'

'I assumed it was because he doesn't want to get his country involved in a war.'

Stern laughed. 'Far from it! President Taft wouldn't hesitate to throw this country into a war; his family would make a fortune. No, his opposition to you, his *Anglophobia* even, has its roots a bit further in the past than the current war. His father ran for president in 1909, but was thoroughly beaten by Carlos Pellegrini, the first Argentinian to hold the office. An Argentinian who was only a second generation American after his grandparents emigrated from England. And who only gained so much support by negotiating with Queen Victoria for the return of the Malvinas islands from Britain. So you can imagine how he can blame British collusion for the defeat and subsequent sharp decline of his father's career and health.'

'You seem to know a lot about him.'

Stern shrugged. 'More wars have been won and lost with correct or incorrect information than force of arms. And I have made a point of studying both friends and enemies alike.'

'I wish I could do that in the air sometimes, but dogfights only last seconds and very often I just have to guess what my enemy is going to do. Unless I'm going up against Hans Gruber, of course; all the Misfits know exactly what he's going to do in a fight.'

'Run away, by any chance?'

Gwen chuckled. 'More often than not, yes!'

'So, how are you going to deal with him? The President, that is, not Gruber! I can't see you winning him over.'

'The plan is to ignore him, really. We're working under the hypothesis that if we win over enough of the people then the politicians will have to vote on our side.'

Stern nodded. 'That should work, but you'll have to win over a lot of people. Far more than you can meet at soirees like this one. And of all classes, not just...' he jerked his head at one of the couples sharing the floor with them with a barely concealed sneer, the woman dripping with jewellery and the man dressed in a long coat covered in what looked like real peacock feathers, 'these over-privileged wastrels.'

Gwen was somewhat shocked at his attitude, especially seeing as he was at the party with those wastrels, enjoying himself just as they were, but she brushed it aside; after all, she didn't know enough about him to question his judgement or motives. 'Well, I'm making an appearance at a few air shows, starting with the one in Philadelphia the day after tomorrow, and Kitty has done a radio show today - I assume there's an audience for that kind of thing.'

'That's a good start. What else?'

'I'm not sure what else we're doing.' She smiled sheepishly. 'We were given a timetable, but I haven't had much time to look at it.'

'I suppose you have been kept quite busy, but, then again, there's no time to waste, what with how things are going. Speaking of which - what will the Misfits do now? Which part of the world are they being sent to save next?'

'Actually,' said Gwen,' the Misfits have...'

'Ah, Squadron Leader, there you are.'

The two were forced to come to a halt as Gascoyne-Beresford suddenly appeared beside them, uncomfortably close.

'Guten Abend, Herr Stern.' The aide nodded at Gwen's dance partner, but then started and looked back and forth between them in surprise. 'Oh, am I in the way? I do apologise.'

Stern's smile turned sour and he glared at the aide. His lip curled into an ugly snarl and he opened his mouth to speak, but then seemed to remember himself and stepped back from Gwen. 'It has been a pleasure, Squadron Leader. Thank you.' He gave her a curt bow, not much more than a nod, clicking his heels together as he did so, then stalked away.

Gwen turned to Gascoyne-Beresford, a question on her lips, but before she could put it into words he had taken her hand and twirled her back into the dance.

'Before you ask, yes, that man was a Prussian.'

'I thought he was one of those "allies" you were talking about - his accent was so American!'

'Isn't Gruber's?' The aide raised an eyebrow and gave her that smile of his that was so charming while at the same time bordering on infuriatingly smug. 'Stern,' he pronounced the man's name as he had before - as if it had an "h" between the h and t, 'is a distant cousin of the Kaiser and has been in America all his life. He was the natural choice to succeed his father as the Prussian Ambassador to the United Federation of American States, when he retired. So, you can imagine my concern when I found you so caught up in conversation with him. I do hope you didn't tell him anything you shouldn't have. Hmmm?'

'No. I mean, I don't think so. We spoke about how busy I've been and my schedule.' She thought back over the conversation. 'I did tell him that our strategy was to get to the politicians by winning over the people, but that's fairly obvious, isn't it?'

Gascoyne-Beresford thought for a moment. 'I think the only thing we really don't want anyone knowing about is the visit to Wardenclyff tomorrow. He might decide to prevent that.'

'Is it that important? Yes, of course it is.' Gwen answered her own question after only a moment, not giving the aide the chance to do so. 'I suppose a better question would be what they could do to stop us?'

'Quite a lot actually.' Gascoyne-Beresford said before breaking off to nod and smile at a couple as they swooped past. He waited until they'd moved on before continuing. 'The Prussians hold sway with quite a few local politicians and many of the particularly vehement anti-

Tesla groups are at least partially funded, if not outright run by them. They could have protesters outside the facility, blocking your way easily enough. Or have it shut down on some pretence or other. They are not beyond using more direct methods either.'

'Direct methods? You mean violence?'

'Yes.'

'Could they really get away with that here?'

'Easily.' The aide nodded. 'So could we, for that matter, but it would be political suicide for us if we were found out, losing us the majority of our supporters, whereas theirs would undoubtedly applaud and congratulate them on their tactics.'

Gwen released him and stopped abruptly, a move which, disappointingly, did nothing to unbalance Gascoyne-Beresford, who merely spun to a halt at a socially-appropriate distance and looked at her quizzically.

'Are...' She began, but then thought better of it; the other couples on the dance floor were watching them surreptitiously. They couldn't have missed Stern storming off and two of them had already altered course slightly in an attempt to get close enough to eavesdrop.

She led the aide off the dance floor to a row of chairs at the side of the room where the only thing that would overhear them over the music would be a statue of what she supposed was Benjamin Franklin, one of the founders of the museum.

'Are Kitty and I in danger?'

'Not nearly as much as you are every time you go into battle.'

Gwen scowled at him. 'So we *are* in danger. Can't you just speak plainly for once?'

'Speak plainly?' Gascoyne-Beresford gave her an exaggerated look of horror. 'Darwin forfend those of us in the diplomatic service should ever speak plainly or,' he gasped, putting a hand to his chest, '*tell the truth*! Then what use would we be?'

Gascoyne-Beresford stayed closer to Gwen after that, not letting her out of earshot, although he did manage to remain fairly unobtrusive and she was fairly sure that most of the people she spoke to didn't notice he was there. However, while the snide remarks and insults continued as before, nobody else of consequence tried to prise any information from Gwen and no further intervention on his part was necessary.

She was kept so busy and shell-shocked by the constant pressure that it wasn't until past midnight, when the party was winding down and Gascoyne-Beresford told her it was time to leave, that she realised she hadn't seen Kitty since just after they'd arrived.

She appeared when they left the museum, though, and all but fell into the back seat of the Consulate autocar, grinning widely and smelling quite strongly of bourbon.

Gwen frowned at her. 'Where on earth have you been? I could have done with some support in there. Or just a hug every so often.'

Kitty shook her head vigorously. 'Couldn't. Had orders.'

'Orders? To get fall-down drunk and disappear all night?' Gwen looked from the still grinning and decidedly unstable American to the aide, knowing that he would be behind her behaviour.

Gascoyne-Beresford stifled a laugh behind his hand as he nodded. 'I did ask Lieutenant Wright to get herself into the kitchens at the earliest opportunity. The people who work behind the scenes often know more about what's really going on than anyone else. I didn't, however, specify how much she had to drink while she was there. That is all her own... initiative.'

'S'right.' Kitty slurred. 'They know *evrrthing*.'

'And I'm hoping you remember it...' the aide said.

Kitty blinked and looked at him. She almost went cross-eyed with the effort of thinking. After what seemed like an age she simply replied 'yes' before sliding sideways in the seat and ending up with her head in Gwen's lap, snoring gently.

Gwen had been to hundreds of *Société Aéronautique* dinners, socialised with university students for three years, and been in the company of RAC pilots for a year or more, but, even so, she had never met anyone who could hold their drink like Kitty. She had drunk an entire squadron under the table when they'd been in Muscovy, tossing back the vodka like it was water, and, when the last of them had slipped into unconsciousness, had just walked away and gone about the rest of her day as normal, somewhat unsteadily, but perfectly capably, even supervising some work on her beloved aircraft, *Hawk*.

It was no surprise to the British pilot, then, when she was woken up in the early hours by the sound of Kitty scribbling furiously on the hotel stationery at the makeup table in their room.

'I take it you got something useful, then?'

'I have no idea. I'm just writing down everything I can remember.'

'Ah.'

Gwen watched her for a few moments. The American hadn't bothered to get dressed and the play of the muscles of her bare back as she wrote was fascinating. However, it wasn't enough to keep Gwen from the embrace of sleep for long and soon her eyes closed and she dropped back into a sleep that had been troubled by oppressive dreams since they'd arrived in the country.

CHAPTER 6

Gwen found Kitty beside her when next she woke, this time at a decent hour with sunlight radiating around the edges of the thick curtains. The American was snoring loudly and didn't stir when Gwen rolled out of bed or padded across the room.

There were about a dozen pieces of paper strewn over the makeup table, each one completely covered on both sides with writing. She twitched the curtains to let in a bit more light and bent over them. Kitty's scrawl was untidy at the best of times, but it had been rendered almost illegible by her alcohol consumption and she quickly gave up. Instead, she gathered the papers, folded them neatly and sealed them in an envelope. It probably wouldn't do to leave them lying around for anyone to see; who knew who wandered in and out when they weren't there - there could be any number of spies for any of the factions present in America among the staff, including their own. In fact, after her encounter with Stern and what Gascoyne-Beresford had said, she half expected the ones in the employ of the Prussians to outnumber the rest by a hefty margin.

'Would you please stop making so much noise?'

The words were about as intelligible as the writing, slurred and muffled by a pillow, and Gwen smiled and went over to sit on the side of the bed next to Kitty, who groaned and buried her head further.

'And close the curtains before I go blind!'

'It's nearly time for breakfast, darling. We're meeting Nicole at eight, remember?'

'Urghh...'

Gwen chuckled and reached out to smooth the American's rumpled hair. Kitty might well be an extremely functional dunk, able to carry out full conversations, play, and win, at poker, and even fly, but she paid the price and was usually incapacitated for at least a few hours the next morning.

It took a fair amount of gentle persuasion, but Gwen eventually managed to get Kitty out of bed and dressed in one of the few sets of civilian clothes they'd brought. She wasn't exactly her usual beautiful self when they went down to breakfast, but she was certainly awake and aware enough to palm the envelope off to one of the waiters in the dining room on the way to the table, confirming Gwen's suspicions.

Nicole was waiting for them at the table up against the window, which was apparently permanently reserved for the Teslas and their guests. She was just as eager as they were to get to the Tesla facility so they ate quickly and it wasn't long before they were bundling into the back of Nicole's autocar, a white machine that dwarfed any they'd seen before, including the king's. It was electric and instead of the occasional loud ticks of a large spring slowly unwinding there was a slight hum coming from the front, but it was covered by the noise of the tyres as soon as they pulled away.

The road was surprisingly wide, remarkably smooth and extremely straight, as unlike Britain's meandering lanes as it could be. The autocar was also very quick, despite its size, so the sixty-five mile journey took less than an hour. Their destination had been visible for the last five minutes of that, though, its famous domed tower looming over the surrounding buildings, and Gwen hadn't been able to tear her eyes away from it. The tower was a symbol for everything a scientist could aspire to - not just success in their work, with the fame and fortune which might come with it, but the journey too, with the obstacles and setbacks that could be overcome with perseverance and hard work.

However, the tower with its steel cupola was no longer the sole landmark, like it was in the photographs that graced so many school textbooks around the world, it was now flanked by two more structures. They weren't the same domed construction, though, they were more conventional in form - a radio tower and an airship mooring mast that rose high above the other two.

The facility itself was far larger than it had originally been as well. The single small brick building that had been Tesla's laboratory for so many years was still there, but it was now surrounded by half a dozen much larger structures.

The autocar pulled off the road and into a large car park. It was quite full already, but there was a space reserved for Nicole next to what appeared to be the only opening in a tall fence which enclosed the entire facility. The opening was protected by gates overseen by a pair of security guards in a small glass and metal hut and Nicole led them through, smiling at the guards as they greeted her in passing.

Next to the gates, up against the inside of the fence, was a row of small four-wheeled vehicles that could only loosely be called autocars, being little more than a black frame with four black seats and a roof to protect the passengers from the elements. A small metal box at the front had to contain an engine, although it was barely large enough to be used for Schrödinger's thought experiment, and there was a domed aerial on the roof.

'Hop on!' Nicole called out, taking the wheel of the first of the vehicles. She stomped her foot on one of the two pedals before Gwen and Kitty were fully in their seats, throwing them back with the sharp acceleration.

The young woman piloted the autocar like a fighter aircraft, swerving and weaving at top speed around any obstacle she came across, whether they were crates, lamp posts, lorries, or even people, at times only missing them by inches. After a harrowing two-minute ride she came to a halt in a screech of brakes outside the original building and turned in her seat to grin at them.

'What do you think? Fun, aren't they?'

Gwen released her grip on the side frame of the vehicle and flexed her aching hand. 'Yes. It's very impressive.' She swallowed the far less complementary comments that she wanted to make about the woman's driving skills, or rather her consideration of the people sharing the roads with her, and instead gave in to her curiosity. 'It's electric, obviously, but the box on the front isn't big enough for the whole motor... Is it?'

The kind of acceleration and velocity that the vehicle had demonstrated would require not only a decently-powered propulsion system, but also a large battery so as not to need recharging every few minutes.

Nicole's grin widened. 'Under normal circumstances it wouldn't be, but the only thing in there is the motor. There's no battery, or any of the other things that an electric motor needs.'

'How...?' Gwen stopped suddenly and reached up to grab the edge of the roof. She used it to pull herself to her feet so she could inspect the domed antenna perched on it. It was like a miniature version of the tower looming over them. 'Wireless energy transmission? Really?'

Kitty, who'd been going greener and greener as the ride progressed, instantly perked up at the words and scrambled onto her own seat to look. 'Your father got it working?'

'Yes!' Nicole said enthusiastically, but then shrugged, her smile fading. 'Well, after a fashion... Which is why I asked you to come.' She gestured at the door they had stopped in front of. 'Shall we?'

Nicole's workshop took up the entirety of the building and, just like the hangar that served as Gwen's workshop at her parent's house, it was filled with projects in all states of completion, strewn around haphazardly. The young woman led them quickly through the maze, pointing out various things distractedly as they went, but not giving them any time to inspect them any closer; her mind was obviously racing ahead of them.

They finally got to the back of the building, where a space had been cleared along the entire length of the wall by pushing the experiments and workbenches that had previously been there out of the way without much care for whether things got damaged. If her dismissive attitude towards everything else in the workshop hadn't been indication enough, the carnage Nicole had caused by doing that demonstrated effectively how important this particular experiment was to her.

She stopped at the edge of the cleared area and turned to them, grinning wildly. 'Here we are.'

Gwen looked up and down the long narrow space. At one end was a sheet of metal, at the other was a mess of wires and cables with what looked like a gun poking from them.

'A firing range?' Gwen said with a frown. 'You've put a firing range in your workshop?' She looked around doubtfully. 'Isn't that a bit... dangerous? I can see at least two or three things nearby that wouldn't react very well to being shot or hit by a ricochet.'

'No, not really. Everything's grounded.'

'Grounded? What's that got to do with...? Oh!' Gwen looked towards the weapon in understanding.

'Exactly!' Nicole cried out, rubbing her hands together in glee. 'Come on, let's fire her up! I set up a fresh target this morning and I want to put some holes in it!'

The young woman and Kitty all but ran to the gun, but Gwen followed more slowly, looking back towards the rest of the workshop as she ran through the mental list she'd made of the various experiments they'd passed. She had no idea what some of them were supposed to do and she wasn't sure why Nicole was even bothering with others, but there had been a few that would be very useful to Britain if they worked. Not just weapons, like what they were there to see, but also machinery that would do things like make manufacturing more efficient, or communications more reliable. There hadn't been any sign of the electrically-powered aircraft it was rumoured she'd built, though, and that was what she'd most been hoping to get a look at.

By the time Gwen reached them, Nicole was flipping switches and peering at dials, babbling to Kitty about things that she mostly understood but wasn't particularly interested in - Kitty was the electrical expert, her interests rested firmly in the mechanical. She stood back and watched them, looking for some remnant of the relationship that they'd had years ago when they'd been at school together, but, beyond a familiarity that went beyond mere work colleagues, there was no real sign of it.

After minute or so, the young woman seemed to finish her explanations and looked up.

'Ready?'

Gwen nodded. 'I am, but is it?' The machine wasn't showing any sign of being ready to do anything - there were no lit indicators and it wasn't humming or making any other noises. It was just sitting there as if it were inert and inoperable.

'Yes. Look.' Nicole swivelled a gauge to show it to Gwen. The needle on it was bouncing lazily around a hand-drawn line labelled "full power" in meticulous handwriting.

'Oh. Alright.' Gwen looked to Kitty for confirmation, but the American was too busy scrutinising the machine, perhaps memorising details for a report to Gascoyne-Beresford.

'OK, here goes!'

Nicole pressed a spring-loaded switch on a panel mounted on the weapon. After a second she released it again.

'Let's go take a look, shall we?' she said, rubbing her hands together.

Gwen blinked at her. 'At what?' The machine hadn't done anything as far as she was concerned.

Nicole laughed and looked at Kitty. 'She's so funny, no wonder you like her so much!' She skipped off down the range towards the target.

Kitty shook her head as she came over to Gwen. She took her hand and pulled her after the young woman. 'What were you expecting?' she whispered. 'Fireworks? Sparks?'

'I suppose not, but *something*, though.'

Kitty chuckled. 'I'll let her explain why there wasn't anything.'

Nicole was standing proudly in front of the sheet of metal, waiting for them, and when they got there she slid to the side to reveal a hole and held out her hands like some music hall magician's assistant. 'Ta da!'

Gwen gaped at it. It was perfectly circular, six or seven inches across and there were no irregularities to it, no burrs or jagged edges like those left by projectile weapons. It looked more like it had been cut by some machine than made by a weapon. The edges were also glowing slightly, as if they'd been heated to an extreme temperature.

'You built a death ray,' she said quietly. 'Your father spoke about this a decade ago and you got it to work.'

Nicole shook her head. 'My father never got his "death beam" to work. He gave up on it when the military got a bit too interested in its possible applications as an offensive weapon rather than a purely defensive one. No, this is all my own, although it does function on the same principles as my father's tower.'

'Energy transference did this? Gosh!' Gwen looked at the hole again. 'This metal sheet has to be three inches thick and it's, what, steel?'

She looked to Nicole for confirmation and the young girl nodded.

'This will rip through Duralumin like it was paper! With this we could...'

'Whoa, whoa, whoa!' Nicole cut her off quickly. 'Hold your horses! Before you get too excited, I have something to show you.'

The metal plate was mounted on an electric cart and she backed it up half a dozen yards.

They returned to the weapon where she went through the charging process again before changing her targeting slightly and firing.

This time she was far less enthusiastic when she took them back to the metal plate and it was easy to see why - the only thing the weapon had done was make a small patch of the bare metal hot.

'Lethal at fifty metres. Little more than a cigarette lighter at fifty-five.' Nicole said. 'It's the same problem we have with the cars outside - as soon as you get outside the fence the power cuts out.'

'Why not just build a bigger transmitter, then?' Gwen asked.

The two Americans both smiled and Gwen knew her limited knowledge of electrical engineering had just let her down and made her say something that sounded silly to them.

'A bigger transmitter wouldn't extend the range, it would just be able to supply power to more cars, which is the problem we're having with all our electrical transmission devices.' Nicole explained patiently, before turning to Kitty. 'This is why I asked you here - I need your help with my baby. I think I can make a version of it small enough to mount on an aircraft, but the range it has at the moment means it's useless.'

Kitty nodded. 'Ideally it would need a minimum of a five hundred metre effective range.'

'Exactly.'

'Good morning, ladies!'

The three women turned to find Tesla hobbling towards them through the chaotic workshop.

'Morning, Grampa!'

'I see you haven't wasted any time.' Tesla went to Nicole and stuck his cheek out for her to kiss, then looked at the two pilots. 'How was the journey? Comfortable? I trust my granddaughter is taking care of you?'

'We're fine, thank you, Niko,' Kitty answered, 'and yes, Nicole is taking good care of us.'

'Good, good.' He looked at Gwen. 'Well, these two will probably be aware of nothing else in the world except Nicole's device for a few hours, so what do you say we go and have that chat?'

'That would be wonderful, uh, *Niko*.'

Tesla laughed and offered her his arm. 'Come on, then. We'll go out the back way. See you later, ladies!'

'Bye, Gramps!'

Even if he was a little unsteady on his feet Tesla's grip on her elbow was surprisingly strong as he took her towards the nearest door leading out of the back of the building. He didn't open it straight away, though, but turned and looked back towards Kitty and Nicole. They were already deep in discussion as they tore apart the electrical weapon.

'What did I tell you?' Tesla said, his eyes shining with mirth. 'I'm afraid they're not going to meet with much success, though; what she's trying to do is impossible.' He shrugged. 'At least, that's what I think. Maybe she'll surprise me, though. She often does.' He winked. 'But, before we go to my office I have something to show you that I think you'll be far more interested in.'

Gwen helped him to open the heavy door and they stepped through. It didn't lead outside anymore, though, because an extension had been put onto the back of the original building. It was a large construction, made with metal girders, which every pilot would be familiar with - a hangar - and there were three aircraft in it.

'These are Nicole's attempts at making an electric aircraft before she got bored and moved on to something else.'

He pointed his cane at the aircraft against the far wall. It was a large biplane. A bomber from the 20's.

'Her first attempt was moderately successful, but all she did was take the hydrogen engine out and replace it with her prototype electric engine. They were similar in weight, so it was fairly easy, however, nobody was interested because the aircraft was already obsolete.'

He pointed at the next aircraft - a military transport from the last decade.

'The military were quite interested in this one and she got it working for them, but it has limited range unless you fill the cargo space with spare batteries, so it was scrapped.'

Instead of pointing at the last aircraft he walked towards it. 'Limited range isn't too much of a handicap for a fighter, so that was naturally where she finally turned. That was her goal all along anyway; she'd always wanted to build something for Kitty to fly.'

Gwen looked the fighter over critically. It was a fairly recent aircraft, by the Hammond Aircraft Engineering Corporation, which they had called the "Andes", after the mountain range. It was stocky, typical of American designs, but from what she'd read about it, it was similar in weight and performance to the Harridan, although it likely wouldn't be quite as capable if fitted with an American spring. That fact made it a good choice for the experiment, though, as the American military would be desperate for something that allowed them to close the gap between American and European-built springs.

'How does it handle?'

'The most charitable things that can be said about it is that it flies. But only barely. Nicole had to pack the fuselage with batteries to give it performance comparable to a spring, which made it almost twice as heavy as it was. I believe the test pilot told her that it handled "like a pig".'

Gwen winced. 'I can imagine.'

Tesla took her arm again and they walked past the aircraft, out the other side of the hangar and into the morning sunshine, then turned towards one of the nearby buildings.

'Nicole got the planes working fine and has proven the concept, but, no matter how brilliant she is, the feasibility of the technology is not in her hands, it's in the hands of people like me who are working on improving batteries. For example I'm working on a sea water battery that we could put into flying boats so we could have them fly uninterrupted around the world, just landing in the sea every so often.' He nodded back the way they'd came. 'Ideally, though, Nicole and

Kitty would solve the problem of energy transmission and we could do away with the need for batteries completely, but as I've already said, that's unlikely.'

'That's a shame,' said Gwen. 'An aircraft that could run both its weapons and engine from the same power source would be interesting.'

'Perhaps some investigation should be done into spring-powered weapons, then?' Tesla said with a grin.

Gwen sniggered. Just before the war broke out, the Prussians had very famously put a lot of time, effort, and money into developing spring weapons, only to quietly brush the project under the carpet when a malfunction in a demonstration - a break in a spring under immense tension - killed most of the scientists, along with one of the Kaiser's cousins, in a horrendous manner. By all accounts, the technology hadn't been very promising anyway.

'What about gasoline-powered aircraft?' The idea of such a thing was distasteful to Gwen, but that didn't trump her curiosity. 'Everybody over here seems pretty keen on using that for just about everything.'

Tesla wrinkled his nose. 'God-awful stuff... Yes, unfortunately people are looking into that, mostly for transport aircraft. Oil is plentiful and cheap and there are vast reserves of it in this country, so of course that would be of interest. However, I don't think internal combustion engines are going to replace hydrogen or springs any time soon; they're just too inefficient and people would be stupid to pollute the air we breathe like that.'

While relieved that the use of gasoline wasn't going to become more widespread any time soon, Gwen was still disappointed. Existing propulsion technologies were wonderful, but they had their limits and true advances would have to come from something else, something different.

It seemed that Tesla's thoughts were closely following her own and he smiled proudly. 'I am working on something myself, though. It's very early days, but it's promising, even if I do say so myself.'

'Really? And may I ask what it is?'

Gwen half expected him to brush off her question. Many scientists would, not wanting to create a rival by giving them ideas, or be thought less of if the project didn't come to fruition, but the old man brought her to a halt and peered around them in an exaggerated manner before leaning in close.

'Electric. Pulse. Propulsion.'

His stage whisper was loud enough for anyone within ten yards to have heard and Gwen laughed at his antics. The legendary scientist was proving to be very different from how she'd always imagined him to be and she found that she wasn't at all disappointed, despite him not being that sombre man in a severe black suit who was so focussed on his work that he had no time for anything else. That didn't detract from her opinion of him, though. If anything it made his achievements more impressive.

Tesla grinned and started walking again. 'I have no qualms about discussing my invention with you, because you are a friend, but at the same time I have no fear of spies or my competitors finding out about it. It is one of the most difficult of the scientific miracles I would have liked to perform during my life and there is nobody else in the world capable of replicating my work, or even understanding it, not even Nicole. I apologise if that sounds immodest, but it is the truth'

'I can well believe it.' Gwen said, smiling warmly.

'Thank you.' He gave her arm a squeeze then went on. 'Despite its complexities, it is perhaps the project that I have closest to completion and I should be ready to put together a prototype in the next year or so. However, while the prototype will prove the concept, there are a few problems in the design which I have not yet overcome. I'm confident that I'll be able to sort those out eventually, though.'

'And do you have any projections for how powerful your engine will be?'

Tesla thought for a moment before answering. 'Instead of giving you raw numbers and boring you any further, let me put it this way - even with the added weight of the batteries a fighter fitted with the engine would be almost twice as fast as your Excalibur.'

Gwen gaped at him. 'And that's just the first generation engine, with current battery technology?'

Tesla nodded. 'And that's just the first generation engine, with current battery technology.'

'Gosh!'

Tesla laughed. 'I was hoping for a damn sight more enthusiasm than just "gosh", but you're British and I'll take it.' They had reached the back door of a building and he brought them to a halt.

'The applications are endless. You are no doubt thinking that it would make any nation's fighters invincible, that their transport aircraft and bombers would go too fast for an enemy to intercept. I, however, are looking further to the future than just this war. One day we will be back at peace and then mankind will look for the answers to questions other than just who has the biggest stick and those answers might well be found in other places. When it does, I will be ready.' He smiled slyly. 'I'm already building a spacecraft.'

He took out a key and put it in the lock of the door, but then paused. 'Of course, if I do get the engine working I'm going to need a "bloody good" engineer to design the aircraft to put it in.' He grinned at her. 'Want a job?'

'Tea, Gwen?'

'Huh? Oh, yes, please!'

Gwen sat in an armchair in the spacious office partitioned off for Tesla in his workshop and gazed around in open-mouthed awe at the clutter, taking in the evidence of a life's work at the forefront of science. Models and prototypes of various inventions were on shelves on all sides and what little wall space was left uncovered had blueprints and designs plastered on it. The model of Excalibur Tesla had mentioned when he'd welcomed them to his hotel was on one of the shelves, behind a couple of clocks. It wasn't exactly a prominent position, but just the fact it had a place in Nikola Tesla's office was enough of an honour for her and, anyway, if it had been in a more obvious place that probably would have meant he'd gotten it out just to flatter her.

In contrast to the mess of the rest of the room, the large desk which dominated the space in front of the long window was completely clear, apart from a blotting board, a couple of photographs in gold frames, a pen holder and a pencil box. It was, however, flanked on one side by a six-foot tall model of the domed antenna and by a Tesla coil on the other and Gwen eyed them warily.

Tesla put a tray with tea and biscuits on the low coffee table in front of her, then followed the direction of her gaze.

'Yes,' he said, 'those are full functional and I've rigged them to give anyone poking their nose in where it's not wanted a nasty surprise.'

'Will it kill someone?'

'No, but it will incapacitate them, while at the same time sounding an alarm to bring my ample security running.'

'You said something about spies before. Do you get many uninvited visitors?'

'You wouldn't believe...' Tesla said as he poured. 'It seems like we have to do a full sweep of the compound every other day. If it's not my competitors it's the government. Or any number of other unscrupulous nations. The Prussians are the most insistent, of course.'

'Because of the war?'

'No not just because of the war - they've been trying to steal anything they can for more than thirty years, ever since I've had something *worth* stealing. It seems to be a compulsion for them or something.'

Gwen laughed, but then felt a twinge when she remembered her orders. 'And, uh, what about the British? Have they been particularly "insistent"?'

Tesla laughed. 'Well, I wasn't going to say... but yes, there have been a few. Not nearly as many as everyone else, though, and they're far more civilised when we catch them.' He placed a cup in front of her then looked up and winked. 'Like you and Kitty, for example.'

He laughed gently when her eyes widened. 'Don't looked so shocked, Gwen. I know exactly what kind of person your Mr Gascoyne-Beresford is. And I know he would have had no qualms whatsoever asking you to do a bit of spying while you're here. I also know that you and Kitty are among the most honourable people I've ever had the privilege of knowing and that you wouldn't do so unless it was absolutely necessary. Or if you felt your duty to your country required it. There is no need for you to skulk about, however; we could very easily have had this conversation back at the hotel, but I asked you here precisely so you could have a look around. So, if you see anything you think might be useful to Britain, let me know and I will do my best to get the plans into the hands of your countrymen. There's no need to go around trying to memorise everything.'

He chuckled again as Gwen blushed, knowing full well that was exactly what she'd been doing. He made no more comment, though, saving her from further embarrassment, and instead merely sipped at his tea, giving her a few moments to compose herself before he spoke again.

'I hope you'll forgive me, but I would like to get straight to business - even though I screen my workers very carefully there are undoubtedly spies among them. If I spend too much time with you then your adversaries might start wondering exactly what is so important for me to talk to you about, rather than thinking that this is just being two people taking tea together.'

'Of course not, please do!'

'Thank you.'

Tesla stood and retrieved a brown cardboard box from one of the shelves.

Gwen sat up and watched him open it expectantly, but instead of some incredible, world-changing invention, the scientist pulled out four cardboard boxes of cereal and placed them on the coffee table.

She frowned at him. 'You're going to solve world hunger? That's a noble goal, but...'

She trailed off as Tesla laughed and began to slice the front off the boxes with a knife.

'The boxes are camouflage. For this.' He laid the rectangles of cardboard out next to each other on the table.

Gwen peered at them, but as far as she could see they were just plain cardboard. She was starting to get a real sense of déjà vu, thinking she was going to look ignorant in front of another member of the Tesla family, when he handed her a pair of glasses with deep red lenses.

'Here.'

Gwen looked at them and laughed. 'Really?'

Tesla shrugged. 'Sometimes the simplest tricks are the best.'

Gwen put the glasses on and bent over the pieces of cardboard again. With the glasses in place their secret was revealed - each held a quarter of an immensely complicated electrical diagram.

'Invisible writing may be childish and simple, but I've refined it slightly and my ink will only be revealed with that very specific shade of red. Be off by only a little and it will remain hidden.'

'And what am I looking at?'

'This is something your parents asked me for. It's the electrical system for the airship they're building.'

'An airship? Why would an airship need...? Oh.' Gwen looked a bit closer at the plans, taking in the scale and sheer complexity of it. 'They're building a Bertha.'

'Indeed. They have actually been working on this for a few years now, but never managed to get it off the ground due to the weight and inadvisability of a hydrogen-based propulsion system. When someone brought home details of the Prussian airship, including its - how shall I put this delicately - *unique* method of powering its systems, they had the missing pieces of the puzzle and contacted me.'

Gwen took one last look at the diagram then shook her head and removed the glasses. 'I'm sorry, I'm not an electrical engineer, I can't make head or tails of this.'

'Don't worry, you don't have to. You merely have to let your parents know the details of how the plans are getting to them.' He turned the pieces of cardboard over. 'Americans eat a lot of cereal and sailors are no exception. Without knowing it, every single one of the transport ships supplying Europe are carrying the plans with them. Your parents need only one box of each of these brands of cereals and the color code for the glasses. I'm sure Mr Gascoyne-Beresford will be able to get those details to them easily enough.'

'Undoubtedly.'

The rest of the conversation while they drank their tea was far more casual. Tesla asked after Gwen's parents, getting her to describe the advances they'd made in the design of the Harridan and especially their new hydromatic airscrew, even though it wasn't his field of interest. Gwen, on the other hand, couldn't help but give in to a bit of hero worship. It wasn't often one met a childhood hero, especially one that had been put on a pedestal as high as Newton or Copernicus, and she took the opportunity to ask him all the questions she'd dreamed of asking him as a girl.

All too soon, though, they had to leave his office and go back out into the workshop. After what he had told her, Gwen was far more conscious of the eyes following them as they picked their way through the benches, past the scientists Tesla employed. There was no way of telling whether the looks were purely out of curiosity or some ulterior motive, though, and she wondered if her visit that day would have any consequences, either for her or the old man.

'And does he have anything that will help us win this war?'

As soon as Nicole had dropped them off at the hotel that afternoon, Gwen and Kitty had been grabbed by Gascoyne-Beresford and spirited away to meet with Lady Cooper in her office. The interrogation had begun immediately, with them sitting in the chairs in front of the consul's desk and Cooper standing behind it, looking down her nose at them.

'Well,' said Gwen, 'the electric aircraft don't work because the batteries are too heavy and Tesla showed me some designs for armoured vehicles, but they have the same problem, so for now they're useless.'

Kitty nodded. 'And unless Nicole and I can come up with something to extend the range of her death ray then we aren't going to get any electric weapons either.'

'Drat,' said the consul, who was deflating more and more as he conversation went on.

'The electrical propulsion unit is very promising, but he might not be able to get it onto an aircraft soon enough to help us,' Gwen mused, 'and as for the ship to take people into space, that's a simpler proposition apparently, but I'm not sure how many Prussians we'll find up there even if he does manage it before the war ends.'

Gascoyne-Beresford and Kitty chuckled, but Cooper just stared at her, not really seeing the funny side, so Gwen went on hurriedly.

'Tesla has some pretty revolutionary energy generation technologies which would really give Britain an edge for industry and research. Implementing them would require a complete overhaul of the entire country's network, but it would be well worth it, even in the short term.'

The consul perked up. 'Well that's something I could definitely take to the king!'

'You might even get a knighthood for it, ma'am,' Gascoyne-Beresford drawled.

Cooper's eyes really lit up at that. 'Yes! An achievement like that would undoubtedly be worthy of some kind of recognition.'

'If there's a country and a king left to award it to you, of course.'

'We'll have none of that kind of talk, John, thank you. I've told you that before.'

'Yes, ma'am.' The aide nodded.

'Was there anything else?' The consul sat and looked down at the papers on her desk, her mind obviously already turning to other matters.

'Tesla did give me something to pass on to my parents. Plans that they'd requested from him.'

'Very well,' Cooper waved her hand in Gascoyne-Beresford's direction without looking up. 'Give the details to John; he'll know what to do.'

The pilots followed the aide out of the office and into his own adjoining one. It wasn't nearly as big as the consul's, although it did have enough room for a two-seater sofa and a couple of armchairs, as well as a decent-sized desk. He motioned them towards the sofa, then went to a side table. 'Tea? Coffee? A sandwich maybe?'

He served them himself, then took an armchair facing them. 'Good work today. A bit of a disappointing result as far as the war effort goes, but good work, nonetheless. And at least now we no longer need to try to sneak people inside.' He looked at Gwen. 'Was his offer of employment sincere do you think?'

Gwen nodded. 'Oh yes. He seemed very keen on the idea. He even insisted that his offer had no expiry date, that he was perfectly willing to wait until after the war.' She turned to Kitty. 'I was thinking...' she began hesitantly.

Kitty laughed. 'Don't be so silly, darling. Of course you can take it.'

Gwen beamed. 'Thank you. I didn't want to assume anything. I know we're planning to come here in my airship and everything, but...'

'But nothing.' Kitty said. 'I was considering working with Nicole myself, so that would be perfect!'

Gwen squeezed Kitty's hand then the two looked back to Gascoyne-Beresford, who had been watching the whole exchange, smiling fondly.

'I'm going to miss you two when you leave. Everyone around here is a bit too business-like for me and it does me good to see what exactly we are fighting for every so often.' He nodded to Gwen. 'Congratulations, by the way. Although you know that you will be expected to use your position for the good of your country and not just for your own advantage.'

'Of course,' Gwen said. 'I wouldn't have it any other way.'

'Wonderful.' He sipped his tea, little finger firmly in the air, then put it down and pushed it away from himself. 'Right, you've had your day of scientific fun and escaped the calvary of two brunches and an afternoon tea in the process, but now it's time to get back to the mission. Tomorrow is the Philadelphia Airshow. It's immensely popular, the biggest and most important after the "Dallas Airfest", with people coming from all over to visit it. It started yesterday in fact, but it's a three day event, with the highlights being on the final day, tomorrow. As with most things American, they've tried to make a bit of a show out of Squadron Leader Stone's appearance. The organisers actually bought a Spitsteam off us for you, which we shipped down from one of our factories in Canada a week or so ago. It was fully checked out before it left the factory, of course, but you'll have time to give it a test run in the morning before taking it up for the afternoon's events.' He grinned and sat back in his armchair. 'They want you to do two low-level passes in front of the crowd, waggling your wings and waving, things like that, then a final third pass with a Corsario on your wing, but I thought this would be another good opportunity to show them a bit more of what you can do. This time in a British machine. What do you think?'

'It will be a pleasure!'

Gwen returned his smile, but Kitty wasn't happy.

'And what am I doing?' she asked grumpily. 'I suppose you've got me on the ground again, haven't you?'

'I'm afraid so. You'll be with the commentators during the flight, supplying them, and the people listening to the public address system or over national radio, with your unique insight. You won't be suffering alone this time, though - Squadron Leader Stone will be interviewed after her flight and then you'll both be in our pavilion until seven, meeting any and all who stop by. To finish off the day and close the air show, they have a charity ball in the terminal building, which tends to attract thousands of enthusiasts from all walks of life. That typically ends well after midnight, so it's going to be a long day, but you'll have the entirety of the next to rest on the airship down to Venezuela.'

'That'll be nice, I suppose,' Kitty said, still grumpy, 'but one of these days I'd quite like to get in a cockpit...'

CHAPTER 7

'Actually, I'm quite glad I'm not going to be flying *that*.'

Kitty had taken one look at the Spitsteam Gwen was going to be flying and had burst out laughing.

The organisers of the airshow had painted it pink. Entirely pink. And not the subtle shade that Gwen very famously used on her machines - that of the sky at twilight - but a rather eye-watering one that looked like it might banish the darkness rather than welcome it.

Gwen winced. 'The poor machine looks like it should be served as dessert, not flown into combat.'

Gwen's comment only made Kitty laugh harder and she met Gascoyne-Beresford's eye and shrugged apologetically. The aide was too busy trying not to laugh himself, though.

Eventually, Kitty stopped laughing and shook her head, grinning wryly. 'I never thought I'd say it, but this almost makes old Wasp look austere.'

'Well, they tried, I suppose.' Gwen said scathingly. 'But they should have just painted one of their Corsarios; they could have had an exact replica of Excalibur.'

'Ah, but that wouldn't have been so "British", or so "Gwen Stone", would it?' Gascoyne-Beresford said, still smiling widely. 'At least you'll stick out from everyone else and they certainly won't be able to miss our pavilion when it's parked outside.'

'John!'

They turned at the shout to find two men approaching from the direction of the office of the small private airfield the British had been assigned for their tests. The one who had called out, the larger of the two, was a rather overweight and balding man in his late fifties, dressed in an expensive-looking three piece suit. He stomped forwards eagerly with his hand stuck out and a wide smile on his jovial face, but the other, a short, painfully thin man in oil-stained blue coveralls, held back, his eyes glued to the Spitsteam.

'Mr Robinson, good morning!'

After shaking Gascoyne-Beresford's hand vigorously, the man looked at Kitty and Gwen. 'These your pilots?'

'They are. Mr Robinson, may I introduce Aviator Lieutenant Wright and Squadron Leader Stone. Lieutenant, Squadron Leader, this is Arnold Robinson, the president of the Philadelphia Flying Club, our hosts today.'

'Lieutenant. Squadron Leader.' The man's voice was gruff as he shook their hands in turn. 'I trust she meets with your approval?'

Gwen nodded. 'I can't wait to check her over and take her up.'

The man smiled. 'I wish I could still fit in a cockpit that small because I'd be right in line behind you. As for your checks - this is Dwight Murdock, our chief mechanic,' he jerked a thumb in the direction of the man accompanying him. 'He was in charge of the team who assembled her after she was shipped down. You find anything wrong he's the man to blame, but he'll also help you getting her fixed up how you like her.'

The thin man, Murdock, looked at them long enough to nod and mumble 'pleasure' before his eyes wandered back to the aircraft again.

Robinson shook his head, grinning wryly. 'He may not be big on the niceties, but he's the best mechanic I've ever met and a dab hand with anything that flies. You're in good hands.' He looked at Kitty. 'I understand you wanted to borrow one of our aircraft?'

'I, uh, well...' Kitty stammered, taken by surprise.

'I requested an aircraft for Lieutenant Wright, yes.' Gascoyne-Beresford interrupted. 'If you have one available.'

'Of course, of course.' He jerked his thumb over his shoulder, indicating the row of aircraft parked up at the side of the airfield. 'She can have one of mine for the morning. Keys are in the office along with refreshments. And if there's anything else you need, just ask Murdock and he'll set you up.'

He offered his hand to Gascoyne-Beresford again. 'Well, I've gotta go. Busy day ahead.' He nodded to Gwen and Kitty. 'Have fun, ladies, and I'll see you this afternoon.'

As he left, he stopped to put a hand on Murdock's shoulder and the small man started and peered up at him. 'Take good care of them, Dwight. Anything they want.'

'Yessir.'

As Robinson walked away towards a large red autocar parked next to the office, Murdock's eyes began to drift back to the Spitsteam, but he caught himself and looked back at them. He said nothing, though, and just stared at them blankly.

'The aircraft, Mr Murdock?' Gascoyne-Beresford prompted.

Murdock's eyes went to him and it seemed as if he was still going to remain mute, but after a moment he suddenly started babbling. 'Oh, yes, wonderful machine. Spitsteam Mark V. Went together like a charm. Excellent manufacturing. Didn't need a hammer once. Just pop it all together and ready to go...'

He looked like he would continue for a while, but Gascoyne-Beresford rolled his eyes and stepped forward. He took his arm gently and guided him towards the aircraft. 'Mr Murdock, perhaps you'd like to help Miss Stone with her checks?'

'Oh, uh, yes. Not that she needs it, of course. The Spitsteam that is. But I understand a pilot must be sure. Not a pilot myself, of course...'

Gwen started to follow the two men but stopped when she realised Kitty wasn't coming. She was gazing at the line of aircraft.

'Go on,' she said with a smile.

The American turned to her. 'But I was going to help you with your preflight checks.'

Gwen chuckled and shook her head. 'Just go. You'll have checks of your own to do once you find one you like.'

'Well, if you insist.' Kitty grinned, then jogged off, the long tails of her leather dress jacket flying behind her. She skidded to a halt after a few steps though, then spun on her heels and raced back. She grabbed Gwen and kissed her.

'Thank you!'

Without waiting for a reply, she ran off again.

Gwen watched her go for a second, enjoying the sight, but then turned and hurried towards the Spitsteam, just as eagerly.

The Spitsteam had flown like a dream, as she'd known it would. She hadn't flown the new Mark V variant before, or its predecessor the Mark II, but there had been big improvements over the Mark I she'd flown in basic training. A new model Ozymandias spring combined with the Hawking hydromatic airscrew gave it far more power than the older models and a few tweaks to the airframe and the distinctive shape of the wings had made it lighter and more manoeuvrable. It still wasn't a patch on a Misfit aircraft, but the gap had closed considerably and she was sure that, with the squadron's enforced time off, that gap would close further. There was a real danger, in fact, that the squadron's aircraft might well become obsolete if they were prevented from being able to continue with their evolution for very long.

It had taken Kitty only a single glance to choose an aircraft from Robinson's private collection. There were almost a dozen, of all shapes and sizes, and Gwen had half expected her to choose a twin-engined heavy fighter, being perhaps the closest in design to her beloved Hawk, the aircraft she'd lost in Malta. Instead, she'd gone straight for the smallest of all of them, a stubby single-seater monoplane painted red, white and blue, which she called a "stunt plane". She had then proceeded to, quite literally, fly rings around Gwen's Spitsteam as they circled over the airfield.

After a couple of minutes of trying to keep up with the American, Gwen had given up and instead concentrated on getting to know the Spitsteam better, working out a aerobatic routine in her mind that would show the machine and her abilities to the best advantage.

It was only when she was running low on tension that she accepted that she had to land. However, instead of going back to the private airfield she had been directed to land directly at the display field.

Bartram Air Terminal was a large passenger facility, just south of Philadelphia itself, right on the north bank of the Delaware River and within sight of the tall buildings of the city. It had been closed to traffic for the day and the airspace in a five mile radius around it declared off limits to anyone not connected with the air show. Grandstands had been built along the river side of the airfield, with enough seating for at least ten thousand people in her estimation, if not more, while a row of white pavilions for the display teams had been set up on the opposite side, next to the terminal building. The British pavilion was one of the smallest, but it was easy enough to spot as it had a flag flying over it and she taxied to it, escorted by display marshals, who made sure that people stayed back and out of danger. Hundreds of people were already wandering the line of pavilions, even though the display didn't start for a couple of hours, and her brightly coloured aircraft drew quite a lot of interest. People came running from all around to crowd up against the protective railings that separated the pavilions from the public and cheers greeted her as she slid back the cockpit. She stood on her seat and waved to them before jumping down and handing the aircraft over to the team waiting to rewind it and get it ready to fly again.

Kitty's stunt aircraft sacrificed range to achieve its remarkable power and she had had to land fully half an hour before Gwen had, consequently, she was there with Gascoyne-Beresford, waiting for her in front of the pavilion. The American was grinning stupidly and Gwen couldn't help but smile broadly herself at the change in her - it was remarkable what even just a few minutes in the air could do for a pilot's state of mind.

'I trust everything is to your satisfaction, Squadron Leader?'

Gwen nodded to Gascoyne-Beresford. 'It is, thank you. I'd forgotten

'Excellent.' The aide checked his watch. 'Well, you're not due to fly for three hours, but you have a meeting with an airshow coordinator to look over maps and log your flight plan in two. You're free until then, though. Refreshments are available inside, but I assume you're going to want to take a look around at all the pretty aircraft, correct?'

Gwen grinned. 'You know us too well.' She looked at Kitty. 'Come on, you can grab me a cup of tea and a sandwich while I get changed, and you can tell me all about your flight while we browse.'

The British had been put near one end of the line of pavilions, with only two between them and the eastern perimeter fence, and Gwen and Kitty decided to walk that way first.

The pavilion next to theirs had a four-engined bomber from the First Great War parked out front, while the one on the end had a small airship tethered to the ground in front of it. The bomber was a true antique, one of only a few left, and kept in tiptop condition by a private collector and the airship was one of a line of new models that were aimed at family transport. Neither of them were really the kinds of aircraft that Gwen and Kitty were overly interested in, so they turned around after a quick look to satisfy their curiosity and made their way back past the glaring pink Spitsteam and the crowd of admirers it was still attracting.

The pavilion on the other side of theirs was one of the largest and belonged to the American Naval Air Section. Four Hammond *Mountain Cats*, painted in a striking blue and yellow livery, were parked in front of it. Dozens of mechanics were swarming over then, while four pilots in blue flightsuits rehearsed their display to the side, moving back and forth and around each other in a way that was at times comical and yet strangely impressive. Gwen and Kitty lingered to watch, but the men finished after a couple of minutes and disappeared into the pavilion, laughing and patting each other on the back.

Occupying the next half a dozen pavilions was the usual mix of civilian and military aircraft that you got at airshows all over the world. This included a couple of "stunt planes" like the one Kitty had flown, a selection of aircraft that had been used in famous flyvies and a massive cargo hauler that ran on gasoline and was surrounded in a black haze of fumes, despite not having run its engines for an hour or more. Japan had sent along a few of its military aircraft and they got a close look at those when one of the Japanese pilots spotted them in the growing crowd and let them through into the enclosure. His English was broken but he was obviously extremely delighted to show off the machines, even though both Gwen and Kitty considered their designs to be rather basic and old-fashioned. He bowed them out after an extremely enjoyable half an hour and they wished him luck in the display and moved on.

Landing a Spitsteam, with its narrow wheelbase and high stall speed, had always been a tricky proposition and Gwen wasn't used to the aircraft, so she'd had to concentrate more than usual. Consequently, she hadn't had much of a chance to look around on her approach and see what other aircraft were taking part in the display. However, it should have been impossible for her to miss what was sitting in front of one of the pavilions near the far end of the airfield, the sight of which, when the crowds opened slightly to reveal it, brought her and Kitty stumbling to a halt - a bright red aircraft that they had become all too familiar with over the last year.

'What the hell is that doing here?' Kitty said.

'Oh no, that's not Hölle, that's a Blutsauger.'

Gwen and Kitty turned and recoiled in unison as they found themselves face to face with a man in a black flightsuit.

'Gruber!' Gwen gasped, but then blinked and frowned. 'Wait. You're not...' She peered closer at the man and saw that his blond hair was pinned in place and he had makeup on to change the shape of his face. 'You're not Gruber!'

'No, of course not!' The man laughed. 'I'm just a Grubalike!'

'A *what?*'

The man's smile didn't waver even a fraction in the face of Gwen's expression, which hovered somewhere between disbelief and disgust.

'A Grubalike! A Hans Gruber impersonator! Here.' He handed them each a pamphlet. 'Please enjoy the show and feel free to have a drink at the bar on us!' He gave them each a wide grin, then spun on his heels and headed towards the nearest group of people admiring the red aircraft, calling out to them. 'Hi there!'

They welcomed him with laughter, speaking with him animatedly, and Gwen shook her head.

'This has to be some kind of joke,' she said, 'I know that America is neutral, but I didn't expect...' She waved her hand at the pavilion. It was one of the most crowded that they'd seen, although whether that was because the people wanted to see the Blutsauger and the two MU9's in front of it or because of the free drinks they were giving away, they didn't know.

'Don't forget that for most of these people the Prussians aren't monsters who have rampaged their way across Europe. America has always been fairly isolated from the rest of the world and we tend to look inwards rather than outwards. And besides, you've seen the newspapers - it depends on who owns it as to if the Prussians are the good guys or the bad guys.'

'How could anyone possibly think that the Prussians are the good guys?' Gwen asked, incredulously.

'The vast majority of Americans *don't* think, Gwen. They believe what they are told. What they see in print, or,' she pointed at the Gruber lookalike, who was with another smiling group, having a photograph taken in front of the Blutsauger, 'on the big screen. To most of these people Hans Gruber is a hero, a star, someone to revere, to look up to. Unless he comes over here and starts shooting up the place that's not going to change.'

There wasn't much more for them to see after the Prussian pavilion - the last two were taken up by a civilian aircraft manufacturer showing of the latest in what they called "Executive Travel Solutions" and the Philadelphia Flying Club, many of whom had come in their own private aircraft and parked them somewhat haphazardly outside - so they turned around and returned to the British pavilion. Gwen was so distracted by the presence of the Prussians that it was only when they got back that she realised she was still clutching the pamphlet the man had given her in her clenched fist. She smoothed it out to look at it, but only got as far as the title, "Fighting for Freedom", before she crumpled it up in disgust and threw it in the nearest rubbish bin.

'Display Control, this is Badger. Ready for takeoff, over.'
'Roger, Badger, you are cleared for takeoff. Have a good show.'
'Thank you, Control. Badger out.'

Gwen pushed the throttle all the way to emergency unwind and released the brakes. The Spitsteam surged forwards, not quite as powerfully as Excalibur, but still enough to thrust her back into her seat and get her heart pumping with anticipation.

She was second from last in the order of flight for the day. It was a great honour, considering that this was the last day and that the final act to close the three day event was the Navy's display team. Consequently, she was determined to put on a good show, especially seeing as the crowd had enjoyed the Prussian offering, which she had to admit had been rather exciting, with the Blutsauger facing off against the two MU9's in a mock dogfight.

The routine she had originally planned in her head was good and would definitely please the crowd, but that wasn't enough for her anymore - she wanted to blow them, and the Prussians, out of the water.

Taking off at emergency unwind wasn't just for fun, it meant that the Spitsteam was in the air with wheels up and approaching two hundred miles an hour well before she was half way down the long line of grandstands. That was more than enough speed for her to launch into a slow roll. It was completely unplanned and more than a little dangerous at barely twenty yards above the ground, but it was particularly impressive and gave her more than enough chance to look up and wave at the spectators while the aircraft was briefly standing on its wing.

She completed the roll level with the end of the grandstands and pulled up sharply. It was a shame she didn't have enough speed to complete a loop, but she did the next best thing by pointing the Spitsteam's nose at the sky until she ran out of speed, then doing a stall turn and plummeting back to the ground. She powered over the airfield, completed two barrel rolls, then pulled up again. This time her airspeed was much higher and she was able to pull up into a loop just before she got to the perimeter fence. Just as she was approaching the top of the loop, right before she was fully inverted, the radio crackled in her ears.

'Unidentified aircraft, this is Philadelphia Zero One, you are approaching a restricted area. Please change course to zero four five.'

Gwen tutted and smiled to herself - some civilian pilot had gotten a bit lost and was wandering a bit too close to the airfield for comfort. Either that or they were trying to get a better look. It was nothing for her to worry about unless they came much closer, which the airfield's traffic controller wouldn't allow.

She continued the loop until the Spitsteam's nose was pointed directly at the ground, then pivoted through a hundred and eighty degrees and pulled up to begin another run in front of the line of grandstands. Her plans were interrupted, though, when an urgent call came.

'Badger, this is Philadelphia Zero One, be advised you have an unidentified aircraft approaching from the north at one thousand feet, range two miles and closing fast. The pilot is not answering and may have problems. They may be attempting an emergency landing, over.'

'Roger, Philadelphia,' Gwen answered, already searching the sky to her north for the aircraft, 'I will finish my run then clear the area.'

'Thank you. Hold at position gamma and we will advise when the airspace is clear.'

'Roger, Philadelphia.'

Position gamma was a holding area a few miles to the east of the airfield where groups of aircraft could gather before making their appearance for the display, unless they were starting with a takeoff roll, like she had. She could orbit there safely while whatever problem the unknown pilot had was solved.

Gwen was just starting her run along the airfield when she spotted the incoming aircraft at her ten o'clock. However, rather than slowing to make a landing it was diving directly for her.

Gwen magnified the aircraft and frowned as distinctive gull wings came into focus - it was a Navy Corsario. For a moment she thought that it was the one that was supposed to be accompanying her on her final run, but that didn't make sense because it wasn't due for another few minutes, and besides, the pilot wouldn't be ignoring the radio.

Some instinct, developed over countless hours of combat, told her that something was wrong and she jerked the stick back and over, jamming her foot down on the rudder, just as points of light winked into existence on the Corsario's wings.

The sudden manoeuvre saved her life, but the yoke still juddered in her hands as several holes appeared across the roundel painted on her left wing.

The American aircraft disappeared beneath her and she twisted in her seat to follow it, spotting it again as it pulled up from its dive. It passed over one of the grandstands, missing it by barely a dozen yards, making the spectators scatter in panic and Gwen blanched as she realised how close it must have come to spraying them with machine gun fire.

'Badger, are you OK? Come in Badger! Badger!'

The civilian traffic controller's voice was loud in her ears and she winced. He would never been in a combat situation so she could forgive his panicking, but she couldn't afford the distraction.

'I'm a bit busy at the moment, Philadelphia. Badger out.'

The Corsario was banking back towards her, but the pilot had made the amateur mistake of turning towards her front rather than behind and it was a simple matter to line up a shot. It was fairly high deflection, but with the aircraft's full profile presented to her it was a shot she could make in her sleep. There was no risk to the public either, because the aircraft had cleared the grandstands and there was only the river behind it.

She pressed the button on the yoke with her thumb, anticipating the buzzing vibration and the exciting roar as the Spitsteam's eight Whiting machine guns fired.

Nothing happened and she groaned as she realised that, in the excitement, she had forgotten that the machine carried no weapons.

'Well, that makes things just a tad harder...' she muttered to herself.

It wasn't so much that she was unarmed and her opponent was armed, it was that the Corsario outclassed the Spitsteam in most ways. Not as vastly as Excalibur did, but still enough to make it so that she wouldn't be able to outfly a half-decent pilot for very long. Even so, she was determined to give it her best shot and swung the Spitsteam onto the enemy aircraft's tail.

'Badger, this is Philadelphia Zero One, do you copy?' It was a much calmer voice that came over the radio this time and Gwen was about to respond to it like she would a British controller when she stopped.

'Kitty? Is that you? What are you doing on this frequency?'

'Yes, Gwen, it's me.'

Gwen could almost hear Kitty shaking her head in exasperation as she asked what she was sure the American would consider an unnecessary question, taking up valuable time.

'There's nobody else here with combat experience and the usual controller's... well, let's just say he's indisposed, so they've asked me to take over. Now can we get on with the important stuff? Like trying to keep you alive?'

Gwen grinned. 'Roger that, Philadelphia.'

'Good. Now, two elements of fighters are scrambling to help you out, but the closest ones available are on the Machu Pichu and the air division's base across the river from it, and they're eighty miles away.'

'That's too far. I can't hold this guy off that long.' Indeed, the Corsario was steadily pulling away and it wouldn't be long before he would just be able to turn back at her.

'You're going to have to, Badger.'

Kitty's tone was professional, but Gwen could tell how hard it was for her to keep it that way and she had to struggle to maintain her own dignity. 'I'll do my best, Philadelphia. Keep me updated, please. Badger out. Love you.'

She released the transmit button before whispering the last two words, not wanting them to be broadcast across the country, and that was the last moment of weakness, of doubt in her ability to survive, that she allowed herself before pushing all thoughts of anything but the coming fight from her mind.

Her opponent might have shown some inexperience in turning the wrong way after his failed attack, but the fact that he was now using the Corsario's superior speed to open the distance instead of trying to outmanoeuvre her meant that he was aware of the capabilities of both machines. That spoke of planning and of someone that had not only calculated the best strategy for the fight, but was calm enough to stick to it in the heat of combat. And that was bad news for her. Very bad.

Ten minutes was how long it would take help to come from New York, but the enemy aircraft would be able to turn for another attack in less than two. There was no way she was going to be able to avoid coming under fire again - if she turned and ran the Corsario would just catch her, however... She glanced in the direction of the city. It would be easy enough to take the enemy aircraft into the man-made canyons of the high rise buildings, easy enough to keep out of a direct line of fire...

She discarded the idea almost as soon as it had formed; the enemy pilot had already shown a callous disregard for civilian lives. She couldn't lead him towards such a heavily populated area.

The point at which the enemy would turn back was fast approaching and Gwen resigned herself to trying to survive at least four head on passes. That was by far the best thing to do; not only was it was the hardest shot to take, because the high closing speed left very little time to do so, but if the pilot was inexperienced, like she suspected, he might get nervous and his aim might be thrown off.

She was running through the various tactics she used in these kinds of situations, when the solution suddenly popped into her head. It was so obvious, really, that she kicked herself for not having thought of it before. All it would need was some luck, some suitable terrain, and quite a lot of fancy flying. The last bit she could handle, she knew she was good enough, but the other two...

The area around Philadelphia was fairly flat, there were no hills, no mountains, nothing that she could put between her and her aggressor. She had already discarded the city as an option and the river wouldn't do either; it was too wide and straight and didn't meander between canyon walls.

Her eyes wandered to what was just passing below her wing and smiled.

'Perfect.'

She banked sharply, hoping to take her enemy by surprise and throttled back to start reducing speed.

'Badger, are you OK?'

Kitty's voice was full of concern and Gwen realised that, with the flat terrain and the height of the control tower, she must still be within sight of the airfield. Her new tactic must seem strange at best.

During her meeting with the airshow coordinator she had pored over maps and aerial photographs of the local area, learning the landmarks for orientation. The biggest and most obvious point of reference, apart from the city, of course, was the Delaware. There were numerous creeks and rivers leading to and from it, quite a few wending their way through the land between the river and the sea to the south. That huge tract of land had been entirely farmland at one point, supplying much of the food for the city, and a few of those tributaries had been canalized - made wider and deeper to supply the massive amount of water required, as well as allow the farmers to transport their produce by barge. As populations had grown, much of the farmland had disappeared, replaced by towns and villages, and the water was no longer needed. The canals were still there, though, closed off from the Delaware and dry, but maintained in case they were needed for flood release. When she'd asked whether she would be able to use them for an emergency landing if something went wrong, the airshow coordinator had told her that she could, that they were smooth concrete and as wide as roads. They were, in fact, mostly used by youths for racing what they called "souped-up cars" - gasoline powered monstrosities.

She was heading for one of the canals now - she couldn't remember what it was called, but it was named after one of those Shakespearean places, like Verona or Venice - but she didn't intend to land on it.

'Still here, Philadelphia, still alive. I have... well, let's call it a plan, shall we?'

'Understood, Badger. Have... fun?'

'Roger that, Philadelphia.' Gwen gave herself leave to laugh before clicking off the transmit button - now that she had a firm idea of how she could survive she could afford a brief distraction and by the sound of her voice Kitty could certainly do with the mood being lightened.

Unfortunately, the enemy pilot hadn't been sleeping on the job like she'd hoped and had turned right after her. He would be within range within seconds, but the canal wasn't far now either.

She throttled back a touch more, reducing her speed further, and took a deep breath. This was the tricky bit: getting into the canal without hitting the sides or crashing straight into the first of the low bridges that spanned its width.

The time came and she banked hard, lining herself up over the canal, then pushed her nose down and dropped.

Tracers streaked by as the Corsario opened fire, but then concrete was rising up on either side of her and they could no longer threaten her.

The walls were high enough to cover her from all but an attack from the rear, but the Corsario was not the only danger she had to worry about now and she went round a bend and found the first bridge hurtling towards her. Visions of her tailplane being sheared off and her crashing to the concrete below flashed through her head, but there was more room to spare under the bridge than she'd feared and it was past in an instant. She forced herself to relax, telling herself that flying through a trench with concrete walls less than a dozen yards from her wingtips was a perfectly normal thing to do and not the act of a madwoman. It was actually far simpler than she'd thought it would be and after negotiating another few turns and flying under another bridge she forged ahead with her plan and throttled back even more. The air speed indicator showed her that she was still going too fast, though - the Spitsteam did most things well, but slowing down wasn't one of them; it cut through the air too efficiently and drag didn't have as much effect on it as it did on most other aircraft.

Throughout all her manoeuvres the Corsario was shadowing her, turning when she did, appearing in her rear-view mirror every so often. Not unexpectedly the pilot hadn't followed her down into the canal, but unless he did he would have to be content with only taking an occasional potshot at her, dipping his nose to loose a few shots before pulling up again and waiting for another chance. That suited her fine, though; a target low to the ground was extremely hard to hit like that and, even if what she was hoping would happen never did, she would likely last long enough for the cavalry to arrive.

Another glance at the airspeed indicator and she smiled grimly. The Spitsteam was finally approaching its stall speed. That was just where she wanted it so she edged the throttle forwards fractionally to keep it where it was.

Now all she could do was wait and hope.

'Badger, this is Philadelphia. Help is five minutes away.'

'Thank you, Philadelphia.'

Gwen tried to keep the strain out of her voice, but it was impossible; she had only been flying in the canal for a few minutes but her nerves were completely frazzled already. There might have been more room in the canal for the Spitsteam than she'd thought there would be, but that didn't mean it was easy. It still required every ounce of skill she had to negotiate the turns, some of which were quite sharp, and the fact that she never knew what was coming round the next bend had her on the edge of her seat. She might encounter a maintenance crew at any moment or...

She pulled up sharply as she rounded a bend and found a brightly painted autocar with its bonnet up parked in the middle of the canal, right in front of her. She managed to catch a glimpse of an extremely scared young man working on its engine before she was over it, missing it by only a few feet.

Tracers searched her out, but she had already pushed the Spitsteam's nose back down and they ricocheted harmlessly off the concrete dozens of yards in front of her.

'Piece of cake...' she muttered to herself, even though she knew very well how close she'd been to disaster - if the autocar had been parked only a few yards closer to the bend she likely would have clipped it and even the slightest of hits would have spelt disaster for her.

Thankfully, she didn't think she was going to have to stay in the canal for much longer. From what she remembered, the waterway described a winding path through the fields nearest the Delaware, but then it began to straighten out as it moved towards the sea and she was fairly sure that there was quite a long straight, of a mile or more, coming up soon. The enemy pilot had to be able to see that and he would wait until then before really trying to do something - it was what she would have done.

She negotiated a couple more bends and then the canal opened up into the long straight. Instantly she saw the nose of the Corsario drop and points of light came into being on its wings. She was ready and kicked the rudder, slewing the Spitsteam towards one wall, then the other. She couldn't do much, but it was sufficient to throw off the enemy's aim long enough for him to run out of altitude. She watched him as he pulled up and regained height, waiting, but still nothing happened.

'Damn,' she muttered. 'Not slow enough.'

There was no way she would be able to avoid his fire forever. Eventually the pilot would anticipate her or, more likely, get lucky.

She was just going to have to risk everything.

She pulled the throttle lever back another couple of notches and opened the flaps a touch, bringing the Spitsteam's speed even lower.

She watched in her rear view mirror as the aircraft began to overtake her slightly, but then the pilot compensated, lifting the nose marginally and opening his own flaps to bleed off airspeed, before swooping down to come into the canal behind her.

'Come on, come on...'

Gwen braced herself as the enemy pilot levelled off to line up his shot. There was no way she would be able to avoid the machine gun fire this time; she was going too slow, too close to the Spitsteam's stall speed to even slew from side to side. Her thumb caressed the radio button, but she didn't press it. Much as she would have liked to hear Kitty's voice one last time, she couldn't make the woman she loved listen to her final moments. They had heard too many pilots screaming the last seconds of their lives away to subject her to that.

Six points of light winked into existence on the Corsario's wings as the enemy pilot opened fire. He hadn't led her nearly enough, though, more proof of his lack of combat experience, and the shots fell harmlessly behind her. He immediately began to pull up, though, adjusting his aim and Gwen held her breath, waiting for the impacts.

They never came as the Corsario suddenly flipped over on its back and fell from the sky.

An almighty crash sounded from close behind her and she sighed in relief, slumping in her seat, then thumbed the radio switch.

'Philadelphia, this is Badger. Tell those boys they can return to base; I've dealt with the big bad wolf. Put the kettle on, Kitty, I'm coming home.'

CHAPTER 8

Gwen landed back at the airfield to find a much different scene to the one she'd left. The grandstands were empty, the spectators having been evacuated through the perimeter fence and down to the river. Thankfully, nobody had been hit by the pilot's indiscriminate fire, but several of them had been hurt in the resulting confusion and were receiving medical assistance.

The pavilions were deserted too, the people evidently evacuated to the terminal building, but they were streaming out as she landed, led by Kitty, Gascoyne-Beresford and Arnold Robinson. She taxied to them and jumped down, even before the Spitsteam's airscrew had come to a halt, straight into Kitty's arms. The American was on the point of tears and Gwen looked at her incredulously.

'I've been in danger before and you never cried then.'

'I know,' Kitty all but sobbed, 'but I wasn't expecting it today. I wasn't prepared. I hadn't said goodbye.' The tall woman swiped an arm across her eyes, then pulled back and straightened her uniform with a quick glance at a large group of journalists who had come out of the terminal building with them. They were being prevented from swamping the Spitsteam by a squad of green clad soldiers with rifles over their shoulders, but they well within earshot and cameras were already flashing. 'What happened anyway? How did you...?'

Gwen smiled and looked at Gascoyne-Beresford who was hovering nearby, listening intently. 'Well, you know that stall strip? It would have saved at least one life today.'

Gascoyne-Beresford had the decency to look a little ashamed, but before he could say anything an American naval officer stepped forward.

'Squadron Leader Stone? I'm Captain Frank Franklin. I command the *Angeles Azules*, the Navy's display team. I have been authorised to apologise to you on behalf of the Naval Air Section for the attack today. It is inexcusable and we will be carrying out a full investigation on how such a thing even happened. We already have someone running the Corsario's serial number to find out where it came from and a team is on its way to the crash site on Mantua Canal.'

Gwen snapped her fingers. 'Mantua! That was the name.'

'Sorry, ma'am?'

'Oh, nothing. Sorry.' Gwen frowned. 'How do you know where the aircraft crashed?'

Franklin pointed to an aircraft that was on final approach to the airfield. 'The Corsario that was supposed to join up with you was watching the whole thing and providing us with commentary over the radio. He wanted to try to help you, but he's unarmed, so I thought it was best that he just watch and if, God forbid, the worst happened, trail the rogue aircraft.'

Gwen nodded. 'That was for the best. Another distraction wouldn't have helped.' She straightened up, standing at attention, or as near as she could with legs that were suddenly trembling uncontrollably. 'I accept your apology, Captain.'

'Thank you, ma'am.'

The man saluted and cameras clicked and whirred as she returned the gesture.

Franklin waited for her to drop her arm before doing the same. He looked like he was going to say more, but Gascoyne-Beresford stepped to his side and spoke up before he could.

'I'm sure that the Navy will keep us apprised of any progress that is made in the investigation. Thank you, Captain, but it has been a rather long and eventful day. If you don't mind we will retire to our pavilion for a cup of tea and some sandwiches.

'Oh, yes, of course. Sorry.'

Gwen gave the captain a nod then turned to go with Kitty and Gascoyne-Beresford, but she caught sight of Robinson standing under the wing of the Spitsteam, staring open-mouthed at the holes in it and wandered over to him instead.

'Close thing, eh?' he said hoarsely, obviously shaken.

'Not really,' Gwen said. 'This is a solid miss as far as air combat goes.'

The man swallowed. 'Really? But you were sitting right over there...' He pointed at the cockpit. 'That's only, like, two or three metres away.'

'Far enough that it might as well have been two or three miles.'

Robinson shook his head. 'I don't know how you can... To be that close to...' He shuddered, but then seemed to gain control of himself and turned to fix her with an earnest look. 'I shall leave the damage as it is and display her in my aviation museum as a reminder of your heroism and the forgiveness you've shown today. You are already the guest of honour, but would you allow me to have her in front of the main pavilion for the main ball tonight, so that everyone can see it?'

'Of course! But, are you still going ahead with the ball?'

'Of course!' he said, echoing her with a smile. 'The Navy are even going to do their display as soon as we've gotten the injured taken care of and the spectators back in their seats.'

'Isn't that a bit callous?'

Robinson shook his head. 'Nobody was killed and we'd have a riot if we cancelled, especially after everyone got to see an aircraft firing live ammunition - they're aviation enthusiasts, they're literally clamouring for more. Even the people who got hurt are refusing to leave until after the finale. 'Which reminds me...' He patted his pockets. 'I've got to get tickets for free entry to the ball to them. It's the least we can do!'

Gwen wasn't quite sure what else she could say and the conversation was making her distinctly uncomfortable so she just nodded. 'Uh, well, if you'd excuse me, I have to...'

She waved vaguely in the direction of the British pavilion then moved off hurriedly to join Kitty and Gascoyne-Beresford.

They had walked a dozen yards before Kitty spoke. 'Not close? If the Corsarios had cannons instead of machine guns you'd have gone straight into the ground.'

'What was I supposed to say? That the enthusiasts, who are not just a little bit crazy, by the way, were unlucky not to have been treated to the sight of me being spread across the runway? I'm sure they would have bloody "clamoured for more".'

'Why do you say they're crazy?' asked Gascoyne-Beresford, who seemed more amused by what was happening than concerned.

'You heard Robinson! They want to finish off the display! They're even going to go ahead with the ball!' Gwen thought that aviation enthusiasts were a strange bunch at the best of times, but what she'd seen of the American ones so far...

'And the people of London last summer. Carrying on with their lives even though bombs were falling on their homes every night? Were they crazy?'

'No. But that's different.' Gwen said, sulking.

'Yes, of course it is.' Gascoyne-Beresford said, implying with his tone that it was anything but. 'It is their decision, though, and we will go along with it. You *will* go to the ball tonight and be the picture of British stoicism, as if nothing untoward had happened.'

'How am I supposed to act normally after someone just tried to kill me? What if someone pulls out a gun and shoots at me? They could kill dozens of people! And me!'

'They are willing to take that risk and we must too, otherwise it might look like we are running away with our tail between our legs. They will be increasing security, though, so I doubt anything will happen.'

'Increase security?' Kitty said quietly. 'Wasn't it a Navy Air Section aircraft that just tried to kill Gwen?'

An hour after the *Angeles Azules* had finished their impressive display, the airfield was declared closed for flight operations and the guests, four thousand of them, were let in for the ball.

The evening was divided in two parts. The first began as soon as the gates opened and essentially consisted of a repeat of that morning's activities, with the guests wandering around and visiting those pavilions that interested them.

The British pavilion proved to be one of, if not *the* most popular attractions. The twin draws of the "Victor of the Battle of Philadelphia", as Gwen was already being dubbed by some of the enthusiasts, and the aircraft she had flown, attracted hundreds of visitors and the small enclosure proved entirely inadequate to their needs. Gascoyne-Beresford had the Spitsteam pushed further out onto the airfield, so that at least some of the crowd would be coaxed away and not block the access to the pavilion, but that did little to ease the situation and Gwen was swamped by over-enthusiastic people. Quite aside from the security problem that posed if there was someone trying to kill her, she was in real danger from being crushed and in the end they installed her behind a desk and enlisted the aid of some of the air show's security personnel to organise a queue. The enthusiasts accepted the change readily, apparently used to such an arrangement, and one of them even told her that she would make a killing if she charged for her autograph, going so far as to suggest that twenty dollars would be a reasonable amount. Gwen felt quite flattered at that, until the man informed her that Hans Gruber charged fifty dollars for his signed photographs.

Kitty was unwilling to stray very far from Gwen's side and she sat in a chair next to hers the whole time, signing the occasional autograph when someone realised who she was.

After an hour, during which night had fallen, the second part of the evening began and everyone, exhibitors and guests alike, was summoned to the terminal building by an announcement over the public address system. Robinson had something special planned for Gwen, though, and, instead of going with the rest of the British contingent, she clambered into the Spitsteam and started it up.

'Display Control, this is Badger. Ready for taxi.'

'Roger, Badger, permission to taxi granted.'

It was a short run along the front of the darkened pavilions to the terminal and she came to a halt just outside of the pool of light surrounding it with her nose pointing towards the building.

She switched off and waited until the airscrew had stilled before calling again, as she'd been instructed.

'Display Control, Badger is in position.'

'Rodger, Badger, wait one, please.'

Gwen sat and listened to the sounds of the party, the band playing dance music and the people laughing and talking. She couldn't really see what was going on with the Spitsteam's long nose blocking most of her view, but she could well imagine the scenes - she had been to far too many of this type of do, with this type of people, not to be able to.

She leaned back in her seat and closed her eyes, letting the music wash over her while she waited. The tune was a popular one from the previous year called "In The Mood", which she hadn't heard for a while - not since the party at Bagshot House before they'd left for Muscovy, actually. It brought back memories of happier times and she hummed along, slapping the sides of her open cockpit and bobbing her head in time to the beat. The band brought it to a premature close, though, and she sat up and opened her eyes as Robinson's voice rang out. She couldn't hear him clearly enough to understand him, but he would be announcing her and more than likely saying something unnecessarily flattering that would have just embarrassed her if she did. She was already embarrassed enough just taking part in something so showy, so she was actually quite glad she couldn't understand. The only reason she had agreed to do this, in fact, was that Gascoyne-Beresford had said it would be good for publicity and she had to agree that the Americans would certainly eat it up.

Robinson's voice rose in volume as he reached the climax of his short speech and then lights went on all around her, searching out then transfixing the Spitsteam like Prussian searchlights. She jumped in surprise as the aircraft jerked and moved forwards and looked out to find half a dozen mechanics pushing on each of her wings. They must have been waiting on the field to sneak into position while she'd been waiting and she blushed when she caught a few of them grinning at her - they would have been there while she had been enjoying the music so enthusiastically.

The men swung her around a dozen yards in front of the terminal, so that she was parallel to it and she put the brakes on, then stood up onto her seat. She smiled and put her hands on her hips, striking what she hoped was a heroic enough pose for Robinson and Gascoyne-Beresford and trying not to show how foolish she felt while she did so.

However, while that was quite hard for her, it was harder still not to gape open-mouthed at the building itself.

She had already been impressed by the modernist palace made of wrought iron and stained glass during the day, but at night it looked like something from a dream. Each of the four façades depicted one of the sky's many manifestations and they were individually lit to best show them off. The Sunrise Façade facing east was filled with reds and oranges, while the Sunset Façade, with bruised clouds and pinks on one side, contrasting with dark blues and purples on the other, faced west. The Storm Façade, facing north, was supposed to be the most impressive, its clouds dark and brooding and shot through with some of Tesla's tamed lightning, but Gwen couldn't see it from where she was, it being on the other side of the building to her. The façade facing her was called the Fair Weather Façade and was predominantly blue, with only a few white clouds to break the monotony, however, it was anything but dull - intricate and accurate wrought iron aircraft, which were part of the supporting structure of the building itself, soared across all of the façades, but naturally there were far more of them on this one, as there would be in a clear sky, and much of the history of aviation could be found among the dozens of aircraft on it.

The inside of the building was just as impressive as the outside, especially seeing as it had to actually function as an air terminal and not just look good. There were two floors, with all the official nonsense of air travel, like checking in and luggage handling, being done on the ground floor, while the first floor was dedicated to leisure facilities like lounges, cafés, restaurants and shops. The roof was also open to the public, though, for viewing the activities on the field, and Robinson had put the dance floor and buffet up there. Most of the guests were up there, but a few were taking the opportunity to wander around inside and the restaurants, bars and shops that had decided to open during the air show looked like they were doing a brisk trade.

The terminal was a masterpiece, as far as Gwen was concerned, and had actually been paid for largely by the Philadelphia Flying Club. According to Gascoyne-Beresford, it was one of the most exclusive flying clubs in the country and numbered many of the most influential men in northern America among its numbers. The club was as much a social one as an aviation one, though, and the members regularly used the clubhouse in the basement, the existence of which was kept secret from the general public, to do business deals.

It was unlikely that anything like that was going on that night, though, what with the amount of people traipsing around the place, but the aide had asked the Misfits to keep their eyes and ears open anyway.

For now, though, Gwen was going to have to leave the spying to Kitty and Gascoyne-Beresford; she was going to have enough on her plate dealing with the guests, all of whom had stopped what they were doing and were crowding the balconies and windows above her, applauding enthusiastically.

She felt drained of energy and all she wanted to do was go to bed, not play to the crowd then spend several hours dancing and being sociable, but she forced herself to do just that, giving them a last wave before stepping down from the aircraft and going to meet the reception committee assembled in front of the terminal. Robinson was waiting with a dozen VIPS, the usual mix of businessmen and politicians, most of whom were members of the Philadelphia Flying Club and he introduced her to all of them before leading them up the ramp that led directly to the first floor.

When the Corsario had fired at Gwen, narrowly missing the grandstands, as many people had been hurt falling over each other trying to follow the fight as had been knocked over in the panic to get away. There had still only been a dozen or so injuries, far less than there could have been. Several of those people had chosen to go home or to the hospital, but half a dozen, including two with broken arms and a teenage boy with a broken leg, had chosen to stay and they were waiting with Kitty just inside the terminal building to meet her. She shared a few words with all of them and signed photographs and the boy's cast, but there were too many other people waiting to be meet her and Robinson soon dragged her away.

After that it was a confusing whirlwind of introductions and short conversations, snatching an occasional drink of water and canapé in between if she was lucky. She danced with a few of the more important important people, recreated aerial battles for groups of enthusiasts, signed autographs until her hand cramped and had more photographs taken than she could count, all while doing her best to give everyone a favourable opinion of the British side of the war. At one point, while she was speaking to a group of politicians, there was a commotion nearby and someone fell heavily against her. She bumped into one of the politicians and apologised before turning to find Gascoyne-Beresford supporting a barely conscious man.

'Sorry! My friend here has had a bit too much to drink.'

The aide smiled at the group apologetically before enlisting the help of a couple of soldiers to drag the man away.

That was the only even slightly discordant note in the entire night, though. It seemed that the Prussians hadn't come to the party, or hadn't been invited, and if there had been any people who sided with them they kept their opinions to themselves.

It was an exhausted, but content Gwen that collapsed into the back of an autocar shortly after midnight and snuggled up to Kitty, but her hopes of snoozing on the way back to New York were dashed when the vehicle came to a halt only half an hour later and Gascoyne-Beresford ushered them out.

'Where are we? What are we doing?' Gwen began, but stopped abruptly at the sight of the sleek white airship tethered a few yards off the ground looming over her. 'I thought we were catching a commercial airship tomorrow?'

'We were,' said the aide as he guided them towards the boarding ramp, 'but after the events of today it's best if we take our leave of New York in a rather more discreet fashion, don't you think?'

'But I'm meeting Nicole for breakfast!' Kitty protested. 'I have ideas I wanted to share with her!'

'I'm sorry, but that's going to have to wait until we get back.'

Kitty grumbled, but started up the ramp nonetheless.

Gwen, however, held back. 'I thought you said we weren't going to run away with our tails between our legs?'

Gascoyne-Beresford smiled. 'We're not running, we are avoiding unnecessary complications.'

'Unnecessary complications? Is that what you call that man trying to kill me at the party?'

Gwen grinned as the aide gaped at her.

'I didn't think you knew. The men you were with certainly didn't notice anything.'

'I saw you hand the knife off to one of the soldiers.' She turned and started to follow Kitty, but paused after a few steps. 'Thank you, by the way. I didn't see him coming.'

'No thanks necessary, Squadron Leader, I was just doing my job.' He smiled and motioned for her to go up the ramp. 'If you wouldn't mind? I would quite like to be half way to Venezuela by dawn.'

Gwen held his gaze for a second, trying to figure out where exactly foiling an assassination attempt came into a consulate aide's job description, but then gave up and just did as he asked.

The airship was a small one, an "executive" model similar to one that had been on display at the airshow. It had seating for twelve in the main lounge, a small office, two bathrooms and four cabins. Two of the cabins had two sets of bunk beds, but the other two had larger double beds and it was in one of those that their minimal luggage was waiting for them. A cockpit was at the front of the gondola and it included a fold-down bed so that the pilot and co-pilot could take it in turns to sleep during longer journeys.

They were welcomed on board by a pair of stewards, a man and a woman, both in their early twenties, who showed them to seats, then offered them hot towels, drinks and food. Gwen and Kitty thanked them and accepted sandwiches and tea. Gascoyne-Beresford ignored them, though, and went straight to the cockpit. Within seconds there was a whirring sound as the ramp retracted and the door closed, then their stomachs plunged as the airship soared into the air.

After ten minutes, Gascoyne-Beresford came back into the lounge. He had a few dozen sheets of paper and was scanning them as he walked.

He smiled as he reached them and held them out. 'Radiofax copies of a few of the evening newspapers. You made a bit of a splash today, Squadron Leader. Congratulations.'

Gwen took the sheaf of papers and started leafing through them. Every single one of the five newspapers had the story of the attack on their front page and she blushed when she saw that four of them had run with the headline "Put the kettle on, I'm coming home."

'That wasn't... I only said that... That was supposed to be... How did they...? That was supposed to be between me and Kitty!'

Kitty leaned across and put her hand on Gwen's arm. 'Uh, darling, the whole fight was broadcast nationally. Everyone across the country heard everything you did and said.'

Gwen groaned. 'Oh, no...'

Gascoyne-Beresford laughed. 'It's a good quote. Not quite Shakespeare, but nothing to be ashamed of.'

Kitty grinned. 'Right! It's perfect! It's typical British understatement, but that takes nothing away from your heroism. I thought it was good at the time, but seeing it in print just makes it sound even better.'

'And if it wasn't any good, the newspapers wouldn't use it,' Gascoyne-Beresford added. 'It's not the headline that's important, though, it's the content of the articles. Two of these publications were on our side already and have naturally printed glowing reports of the fight and the ball. Two of them were on the fence, but have reported favourably, especially about how nice you were to the injured. The last was, and still is, against us. They don't use your words as their headline or even have the story on the front page. They do cover the airshow, but only on page fifteen and dedicate more words to the popularity of the Prussian pavilion than to the attack. Which they blame you for, by the way. They go on a bit of a rant in the editorial column, saying that you are "antagonising the American people" and that you drove a decent young man to "take extreme measures in an attempt to put an end to the corrupting influence of British tyranny and apostasy".'

'Hang on.' Kitty said, fishing in a pocket. 'That's what's written on this.' She pulled out one of the pamphlets they'd been given by the "Grubalike". 'Almost word for word.'

She handed it to Gascoyne-Beresford who scowled at it. 'They were handing this out at the Prussian pavilion?'

Both Kitty and Gwen nodded.

The aide shook his head and sighed. 'I'm surprised Robinson allowed this kind of shameless attack on us. Perhaps he's not such a good friend after all...' He folded the pamphlet carefully then put it his inside breast pocket of his jacket. 'Well, they may have struck first, but we had the last laugh, as the newspapers prove. Things are looking very good for us and as long as we put on a good showing in Venezuela we should be home free for the vote next week.'

He stood and looked down at them. 'Now, I don't know about you, but I need some sleep. It's a twenty-two hour journey to Caracas because we're taking a rather indirect route, so I suggest you rest, relax and eat well because there may not be time for much of that while we're there.'

CHAPTER 9

The airship set down after dark the next day in an empty field some fifty miles or so from Caracas, the American capital. It had been a luxurious flight, with excellent food, comfortable beds and as much decent British tea as Gwen could ever want. The vessel was a few years old, but was one of the more expensive models, being fast, quiet and extremely well appointed. When they asked Gascoyne-Beresford who it belonged to he merely told them "a friend" then refused to elaborate.

A nondescript black autocar was waiting for them, parked to the side of the field, up against the hedge that divided it from a dirt track. There was no driver, but Gascoyne-Beresford got behind the wheel himself and pulled away smoothly. He seemed to know precisely where he was going because he didn't hesitate once as he followed the winding track. After ten minutes they came to a junction and he turned onto a tarmacked road and accelerated towards the glow on the horizon that was the city.

They hadn't gone more than twenty miles before he turned off again, though, this time onto a gravel driveway. He slowed to a crawl and turned the autocar's lights off, but there was enough light from the moon for him to see well enough at the speed at which they were going. A mile or so up the driveway, past several orchards and a couple of fields, they caught sight of a white stone farmhouse, glowing faintly in the moonlight.

There were no lights on in the house, but Gascoyne-Beresford pulled up behind a copse of trees and turned to them. 'Stay here.' He took his umbrella from the seat next to him before getting out and strolling through the copse.

Gwen and Kitty watched him cross the small garden and walk up to the house, swinging his umbrella nonchalantly. His attitude changed completely at the door, though, as he flattened himself against the wall beside it before reaching out to lift the latch with the point of the umbrella. He pushed the door open with it, then spun through the gap and disappeared.

'Consulate aide my ass.' Kitty muttered.

Gwen looked at her in shock, then burst out laughing.

After a few minutes, the aide came out of the door and returned across the grass to the autocar.

'All clear,' he said as he slipped back into the driver's seat. Without any further explanation he put the vehicle into gear and took them up to the house. He parked next to a tractor in a covered area around the back and they got out and took their bags out of the boot.

'Right, we'll be safe here until the morning, then we'll make our way straight to the Senate building.'

Kitty frowned. 'I thought my speech wasn't until the afternoon?'

Gascoyne-Beresford smiled. 'It isn't, but nobody will dare touch us there and besides the Ambassador is going to meet us and show you around, which will give you a chance to make an impression beforehand. Don't worry, you won't get bored, or hungry - there is also an extremely good restaurant for politicians and their guests and an extensive reading library that has all the latest novels, as well as texts on subjects such as aviation and electrical engineering.'

He pulled a couple of clockwork torches out of his bag and gave them one each. 'There's a gas stove in the kitchen in case you want to make tea or feel peckish, but please use these, I'd rather not turn any lights on.'

He switched a torch on himself and took them inside.

'Your bedroom is the first on the left at the top of the stairs. The bathroom is the door next to it.' He pointed the torch to show the way, then swung it back to the ground floor. 'Kitchen is over there. The cupboards are fully stocked, help yourself to whatever you want. Goodnight!'

He put his bag against the wall, then turned and was halfway out of the door before they could react.

'You're going?' Gwen asked.

'I'll be around,' he answered with one of his smiles. 'If I don't see you before, dress uniforms and ready to leave at ten, please.'

He gave them a nod, then slipped out of the door, closing it behind him.

The two pilots shared a look, then trudged up to their room, neither of them feeling much like anything apart from sleep.

They woke the next morning refreshed and ready for the challenges of the day. They hadn't heard Gascoyne-Beresford come back during the night, but when they got downstairs they found him in the kitchen preparing food. He was wearing the same suit as he'd had on the previous day, now slightly creased, and there was a neatly folded blanket on a sofa in the adjoining lounge, but he looked as fresh and awake as ever.

'Morning!' he called out cheerfully. 'Bacon sandwiches will be ready in a moment. There's fresh coffee and a pot of tea brewing on the table. Please help yourselves.'

They sat at the small table in the kitchen and poured drinks, then tucked in to the sandwiches when Gascoyne-Beresford brought them over. He helped himself to just one, then wiped his fingers on a napkin and sat back.

'The navy have found out who was flying the aircraft.'

'Did the Prussians steal it?' asked Gwen.

The aide shook his head. 'I'm afraid not. It was flown by its regular pilot, a Lieutenant Frank Henderson.'

'Oh.' Gwen said, slumping in her seat. She had been holding out hope that it hadn't been an American who had attacked her, but a Prussian agent.

'However, they have been digging into Lieutenant Henderson's doings and, even though the investigation is in its early days, they have already found quite a few unpleasant things. They include, but aren't limited to, being a member of a religious group that condemns the Kingdom of Britain as heretical and also of an organisation called the *Prussian American Bund*, which actually wants America to become part of the Prussian empire. As part of the Bund he has been to political meetings run by the Prussian government and attended rallies of the style they have organised on a massive scale in Berlin. He even met the Kaiser while he was in Berlin on leave.'

'I've heard of the Bund.' Kitty said. 'They've been around for years. When they first started spouting their nonsense there were protests, especially at their rallies in New York. They provoked them, in fact, to gain publicity. But the protests started dying down when the government not only didn't crack down on them, but sent the police out to protect them and prevent the protesters from getting anywhere near them. It's not just Prussian Americans who joined the Bund either, plenty of other Americans did too, if I remember right.'

Gascoyne-Beresford nodded. 'As Lieutenant Henderson proves. And now, they're actually an official political party, with a couple of congressmen on the books. That has done nothing to make them any more respectable, though, and they continue to spout their extremist and racist ideals.'

He consulted his chronograph. 'Well, this discussion, however informative, will have to wait for another time. I'm going to go do one last check of the grounds.' He pushed back his chair and stood. 'When you've finished just leave everything where it is and get ready. We'll leave in fifteen minutes.'

He picked up his umbrella and went out of the back door.

'And another thing!' Kitty said. 'What's with the damn umbrella? It's high summer and it hasn't bloody rained since we got here!'

They were ready when Gascoyne-Beresford returned and piled straight into the autocar. He drove down the driveway slowly, looking around unceasingly as he did, but evidently didn't see anything untoward and when they got to the main road he pulled onto it directly and accelerated sharply.

He continued to take precautions throughout the journey, making random turns and even reversing course a couple of times while constantly checking the mirrors and scrutinising every vehicle they crossed paths with. Even so, they reached the Senate after about an hour and he threw the keys to one of the men managing visitors' vehicles and rushed them up the steps of the huge white marble building to the main doors. Only when they were inside and through the security checks did he relax his vigilance, but even then not by much.

'You seem almost disappointed that there hasn't been some kind of incident.' Gwen pointed out as they walked the wide corridor leading to the private chambers at the rear of the building where they were due to meet the British ambassador.

'Not disappointed, but I am frankly surprised that they haven't made another attempt on... Oh dear.'

The aide stumbled to a halt, ungainly for the first time since they'd met him and Gwen looked around.

'What? What is it? Have you spotted an assassin?'

'No, worse.'

He stood, stock still, staring down the corridor and the two pilots followed his gaze.

A gaggle of men were coming towards them, tough-looking black-suited young men surrounding five older men in dark grey suits. In the middle of the group walked the president and next to him was Stern, the Prussian ambassador.

The president smiled when he caught sight of them and made a beeline directly for them.

'Ah, Miss Stone, Miss Wright, I'm surprised to see you here.'

'Why is that?' asked Kitty, 'I'm due to address the senate this afternoon.'

Taft laughed. 'I'm sorry, did anyone not inform you? You won't be doing that anymore; that session has been replaced with a budget debate.' He turned to Gwen and grinned. 'I did tell you that you should go home and now you've wasted even more of your time coming all the way down here.'

'What about Senator Rodriguez's report?' Gascoyne-Beresford asked. 'I thought the senate passed a resolution not to make a final decision before he'd had the chance to present his conclusions.'

'Ah, poor Senator Rodriguez,' the president said, briefly hanging his head in sorrow before smiling at them again. 'We received word yesterday that his ship had gone down with all hands, so this morning I proposed that we delay no longer and take the vote. That is what we have done and I am afraid we decided that we cannot in all conscience join the war on the side of the British. We will in fact be signing a non-aggression pact with the Prussian government,' he nodded at Stern, who looked very much like the mouse who had gotten the cheese. 'Someone will of course inform your ambassador of the terms of the pact when they have been agreed upon, at least where it concerns the relationship between our two nations, but I am already quite sure it will mean that we will no longer be providing safe harbour to British ships. Or sending any more supplies, military or otherwise, to the British Empire.'

He grinned. 'Now, if you'll excuse me, I have important things to do. Have a nice day.'

He continued walking and the British had to scurry out of the way as the man's bodyguard advanced on them menacingly.

The group soon disappeared, heading towards the entrance at the front of the building.

'Well, now we know why it was so easy to get here.' Gascoyne-Beresford sighed. 'Come on, the ambassador is expecting us.'

The ambassador's office was in an uproar. They had been taken as much by surprise by that morning's senate vote as the new arrivals and the ambassador was dictating angry letter after angry letter to those senators who were supposed to be supporters, asking them why they hadn't done anything to prevent it, or indeed warn them.

When they made their presence known, the ambassador, a balding and decidedly overweight man in his sixties, who was getting redder and redder and perspiring more with each moment, looked them up and down with a sneer.

'No bloody use now, are you? Be on the bloody boat home in a week, until then I don't bloody care what you bloody do.'

He dismissed them with a wave before turning back to his beleaguered secretary and returning to his ranting.

Gascoyne-Beresford led them from the room without a word or an attempt at deference to the man's rank. His knuckles were white on the handle of his umbrella as he marched ahead of them, back the way they'd come. He stopped suddenly once the noise coming from the offices had faded, though, and turned to them. His expression was normal, but his voice, barely more than a growl, betrayed his frustration and anger.

'I don't know about you two, but I need a cup of tea.'

The restaurant wasn't very busy at that time of day and it was easy enough to find a quiet corner out of the way and order tea, coffee and pastries from a passing waiter.

Gascoyne-Beresford remained silent and brooding until the tea came and he had taken his first sip.

'That's a bit better.' He put the cup back on the table and sighed contentedly. When he looked back up at them he seemed his usual unflappable self. 'Sorry about that, but sometimes the whole politics side of things can become a bit overwhelming. Things were much simpler when I was just...' He stopped himself and just smiled enigmatically, then took another sip before pushing his cup away.

'Well, it looks like your services are no longer needed by His Majesty's Ambassador to the United Federation of American States and I will see to cancelling your remaining engagements. Squadron Leader, I'm sure you won't mind my acting in your name and sending your regrets to the Kansas Knitting Club, the Housewives Society of

Caracas and the various other women's societies you were due to speak at?'

'Not at all, please do.'

'And Lieutenant, I'm assuming you *won't* be cutting the ribbon to open a new leisure complex here in Caracas tomorrow?'

'I'd really rather not.'

'Good choice.' He nodded, smiling warmly. 'Now, as the ambassador said, you have a week before the HMS Beagle is due and your time is your own. I will, however, say that, just because the matter has been resolved in favour of the Prussians, you are not safe. They would still very much like to see you dead before you can get back into the sky and cause them more trouble, so I think it would be best if you stay under the radar, so to speak, as much as possible. I have two days before I have to be back in New York, but I can see you settled in a place like the farmhouse we stayed in last night before then, if you'd like.'

Kitty looked at Gwen. 'Perhaps we could go and visit my family? We'd be safe enough there for a week and I don't know about you, but some rest and home cooking sounds quite good about now...'

Gwen took Kitty's hands and smiled. 'That sounds perfect.'

Gascoyne-Beresford sat back in his chair and beamed at them happily. 'Wonderful! Just don't wear your uniforms when you're out and about and, Squadron Leader, try not to be too British.'

'OK, sure thing!'

Gwen's attempt at an American accent had both Kitty and Gascoyne-Beresford wincing and she chuckled even as she cringed herself. 'Alright, I'll let Kitty do the talking.'

The aide nodded sincerely. 'That would probably be for the best.' He waited until the pilots had finished their drinks then took hold of his umbrella. 'Right, well, there's no point in hanging around this place any longer. Let's get you to your hotel. We can make travel arrangements from there.'

It was a short drive to where they were staying, another of Tesla's hotels, the A.C. Caracas. It was one of the most prestigious hotels in the city and was used by many visiting dignitaries. That included the king himself, the last time he'd been in America, back when he had still been Emperor George II, and the Teslas had made sure that the pilots would have the room he'd stayed in, which had been renamed the "George Suite" in his honour. It was on the top floor and they left the keys to the autocar with the concierge so that he could arrange for their luggage to be brought up and caught the elevator.

The pilots were feeling dejected after the failure of their mission, but they weren't unhappy that it afforded them the possibility of seeing Kitty's family. They were all for leaving immediately and catching the next train to Columbus, but Gascoyne-Beresford had insisted that they at least rest and have a meal before he took them to the station. They had barely gotten through the door of their room, though, before the aide spun in place and pushed them roughly against the wall. He continued his spin in a fluid motion and there was a flash of silver as a sword appeared in his right hand even as a gun materialised in his left.

'Please, Mr Gascoyne-Beresford! We mean no harm!'

It was only when the voice called out that Gwen registered the fact that there were three men in the room already, in the lounge that was just inside the door. One, the man who had spoken, was sitting in an armchair facing them, the other two were standing behind him on either side. All three were Asian.

'Sato-san, what a surprise.' Gascoyne-Beresford said without straightening from his fighting crouch. 'Can we help you?'

The man in the armchair smiled enigmatically. 'It is not what you can do for me, but what I can do for you.' He motioned to the other chairs in the room. 'Please, would you join me for tea?'

He signalled to his men and they bowed to him, then moved slowly, carefully past the aide and the two pilots, bowing to them in passing, and left the room. Only then did Gascoyne-Beresford straighten up and put his weapons away.

'*That's* what the umbrella is for,' Gwen hissed to Kitty with a grin as they followed the aide towards the armchairs.

The man stood as they arrived and Gascoyne-Beresford bowed to him.

'Sato-san, this is Squadron Leader Stone and Lieutenant Wright. Squadron Leader Stone, Lieutenant Wright, this is Hikaru Sato, His Imperial Majesty's Ambassador.'

Sato bowed to the two pilots in turn. 'Very pleased to meet you. Squadron Leader, Lieutenant. Please forgive the cloak and dagger, but given recent events I thought it best not to draw undue attention to our meeting.' He pulled a stiff white card from his pocket and bowed over it before holding it out to Gwen in two hands. 'I have come to extend His Majesty's invitation to you both, to join him in Kyoto to discuss a formal alliance between Japan and the Kingdom of Great Britain.'

EPILOGUE

The pilots were spirited out of the hotel at three the next morning by two Japanese men and taken to a nearby airfield where a light aircraft was waiting for them. Spring-powered, with a short body and long wings, it was a rather strange looking craft that was not quite a transport aircraft or a passenger aircraft. It had no room for anything but the most basic of luggage and only two passengers in addition to the pilot and co-pilot, however, it was good enough to get them out of Caracas quickly and quietly.

Gascoyne-Beresford had accompanied them and he leaned on his umbrella while they waited for Gwen and Kitty's luggage to be loaded.

They watched for a while, but then Gwen turned to Gascoyne-Beresford. 'This is goodbye, then.'

'Indeed it is, Squadron Leader.' The aide gave her one of his knowing smiles. 'Even though things haven't turned out quite the way we would have liked them to, you've done a bloody marvellous job and you've done Britain proud as well.'

Gwen shrugged. 'It's good of you to say so, but we failed.'

Gascoyne-Beresford shook his head. 'You mustn't look at it that way. This is not over. Politicians come and go, but the example you've given the American people of British dignity and capability will last for a long time. And so will the example of what the Prussians are willing to do to get what they want. Things will change. Maybe not today or tomorrow, but someday they will. Thanks in great part to you two.'

One of the men who had driven them approached and bowed. 'It is ready, please to board.'

The aide nodded to him. 'Thank you, they'll be right with you.'

The man bowed again, then went to stand by the door of the aircraft.

'Oh, two things before we go.' Kitty fumbled in her pocket and pulled out an envelope. 'Here.' She held it out to Gascoyne-Beresford. 'Here are the ideas I had for Nicole Tesla. Would you give this to her, please?'

'Certainly, Lieutenant.' He took the envelope from her. 'And I will endeavour to open a line of communication so that you can continue your collaboration. In the interest of science, even if we don't obtain any new weapons from it.'

'That would be appreciated, thank you.'

'You're welcome.' He nodded to her. 'And the second thing?'

'The second thing is... There's no way you're a consulate aide! What are you really? A spy?'

The aide smiled slowly. 'I am whatever I am needed to be.'

'Well you *were* needed, Mr Gascoyne-Beresford; Gwen told me about the man at the party.' Kitty said, then frowned. 'Is that even your real name, by the way?'

'Part of it, at least.' The aide gave them a conspiratorial smile. 'I come from one of those English families that give their scions more names than they know what to do with and I pick and choose. Enough about me, though, it's time you were off; you don't want to keep the Emperor waiting. I will make sure the people who need to know are informed of where you're going.'

'The ambassador?' Gwen asked.

'Heavens, no! I mean the king!' Gascoyne-Beresford laughed then held out his hand. 'Safe journey, Squadron Leader, Lieutenant, and I wish you every success.'

They shook his hand, then went up the steps into the aircraft. The driver closed the door behind them from the outside, but there was another Japanese man waiting in the cramped space inside and he bowed to them before gesturing to the two passenger seats.

'Please sit and strap in, we will take off as soon as you are ready.'

Gwen did up her straps, then leaned across Kitty to look out of the window to where Gascoyne-Beresford was standing. He saw her and grinned widely, raising his umbrella in salute, and she lifted her hand to return it, but in that moment the aircraft lurched forwards and he was left behind, so she couldn't be sure he'd seen it.

She let the mild G forces of the aircraft surging into the air push her back into her seat and closed her eyes as tiredness overcame her.

Something occurred to her, though, and she turned to Kitty. 'What are you going to do now?'

'What do you mean?'

'If America signs a non-aggression pact with Prussia then your status is going to change. They'll stop you fighting for us.'

Kitty shrugged. 'They can try.' She thought for a moment. 'I suppose I could always ask the king to make me a British citizen.' She gave Gwen a pointed look. 'Or I can marry one.'

Gwen blinked at her, surprised. The American had never mentioned making their relationship formal before, even jokingly. She had to admit it didn't sound too bad, but there was no way she was going to let her get away with springing it on her like that. 'Hmmm, Mrs Kitty Hawking does have a good ring to it...'

It was Kitty's turn to stare. She opened and closed her mouth several times, but no words came out. After a few seconds she smiled, though, and leaned in to put her face only inches from Gwen's. However, whatever comeback she was going to make went unsaid when she suddenly frowned and turned away to look out the window. 'We're still climbing. Why are we still climbing if we're just going to another airfield or a port?' She craned her head to peer down. 'We're out over the sea and heading east.' She gave Gwen a puzzled look. 'This aircraft can't make it all the way to Japan, can it?'

The man who had welcomed them aboard turned in his seat and smiled reassuringly. 'Please, do not be alarmed. We are almost at our destination.' He spoke to the pilot in rapid Japanese and received an equally rapid reply. 'We should see her in three minutes.'

'Her?'

The man nodded, as if he'd explained everything and turned back to the controls in front of him, paying particular attention to a small box mounted on top of the instrument panel.

The aircraft went into a cloud as it rose, but burst through only a minute or so later into clear air and an expanse of white, glimmering in the moonlight spread out all around the aircraft. It was beautiful and something that most people, even the majority of pilots, didn't ever see, but the four people in the aircraft had eyes only for the immense dark shape looming directly in front of them.

'Gosh,' Gwen barely managed to get out, her mouth very dry all of a sudden. 'That's the Yamato.'

The co-pilot turned in his seat again as the pilot contacted the airship and began docking procedures. 'Quite right, Squadron Leader Stone, she is indeed the Yamato. The emperor has instructed me to bid you welcome to his flagship and he hopes that you will be comfortable in his own humble quarters for the journey to Japan.'

Gwen nodded solemnly. 'We thank his majesty for his consideration.'

The co-pilot nodded back then returned to his job.

'Um, I'm going to need help with all this protocol stuff.' Kitty said quietly. 'Is it too late to go back for Gascoyne-Beresford?'

Gwen chuckled. 'Just do what I do.' She winked. 'And try not to be too American.'

'Hey!' Kitty scowled. 'Just as well I love you, otherwise I might take offence.'

Gwen reached out to take the American's hand. 'I love you too.'

There was far more that they wanted to say, that they needed to say, but it would have to wait because right at that moment the aircraft was on final approach and they watch enthralled as the pilot matched speed with the airship and prepared to hook on.

Less than a week after they'd arrived in America to fanfares and widespread acclaim, they were leaving by the back door, unwelcome and unnoticed, their mission a failure.

America wasn't the only powerful country not to have declared for either side, though, and Japan had just as much to offer if they became allied with Britain.

Whether that ended up happening or not, thought Gwen, remembering the time she'd spent in Kyoto with her parents, at least they were going to be made far more welcome.

ABOUT THE AUTHOR

Simon Brading's interest in aviation began when he was very young and at thirteen he joined the RAF section of the Combined Cadet Forces of Dulwich College with the aim of becoming a pilot. However, when he was 18, had reached the rank of Flight Sergeant in the CCF and was trying to get into a University Air Squadron, he was told that his eyesight wasn't good enough to be a pilot, so he had to move onto plan B... something else.

He tried his hand at many things before it occurred to him that he might have a few stories to tell. He never lost his interest in flight, though, and hopes to add a PPL to his very basic and probably extremely expired glider license.

www.simonbrading.co.uk

For news of special offers, upcoming releases, exclusive content, competitions and events, please follow me on social media.

Instagram - @sibrading
Facebook - Simon Brading Author
Tiktok - @SimonBradingAuthor

In addition, souvenirs and merchandise, including T-shirts, badges, stickers and more, are available from the Misfit Squadron store on REDBUBBLE at -
https://www.redbubble.com/people/misfitsquadron/shop

ALSO BY SIMON BRADING

The "Displacers" series - a young adult time travel adventure series for all ages.
The Time Traveller's Nephew
The Secret of the Ancients
The Whitechapel Plot
The Price of Greed
The Time for Vengeance

The "Misfit Squadron" Series - a Steampunk series set in an alternate World War 2.
The Battle Over Britain
The Russian Resistance
A Misfit Midwinter
The Lion and the Baron
The Maltese Defence
Tales From the Second Great War
The Siege of Gibraltar
The King's Mission
The Home Front

The Dismal Futures books - stand-alone science fiction tales suitable for adults.
Empath
The Lifeboat at the End of the Universe

The "Twin Ambitions" series - ballet books for children ages 7 and up.
Fight to Dance
Back to Basics

The "Ni Hon - The Two Books" Series - a young adult series set in a dystopian future Japan.
The Black Book

Others
Public Enemy